THE LOST MYSTIC

Tacori Bean

This is a work of fiction. Any places, names, unusual, or historical happenings, are either a product of the author's imagination or used fictitiously. Any resemblance to any places, persons, dead or alive, events, business, locations, or historical happenings, are a complete coincidence.

THE LOST MYSTIC ~ Book Two of The Mystics Trilogy
Copyright © 2020 by Tacori Bean
Cover design by germancreative
All cover art copyright © 2020
All Rights Reserved
Print ISBN: 9781653001828

All rights reserved under the International and Pan-American Copyright Conventions. No part of this book may be reproduced or transmitted, digital, written, or photocopied without written permission from the author, with true signature.

ABOUT THE PRINT: If you receive a copy of this book without a cover, it is stolen property. Please report this if you encounter such a possibility.

Genre: Fantasy-Adventure

~ Dedications ~

Dedicated to everyone who feels like a broken piece of a puzzle. You are not alone. When we stand together, our brokenness makes us whole and we create a light to guide and inspire others like us.

"We are all broken, that's how the light gets in."
~Earnest Hemingway

~1~

DAMON WAS GONE, yet after less than two weeks it seemed as though everyone had already moved on… or maybe I was dwelling too much on a dead man.

Tears began to slip down my cheeks in silent waves at the very thought of him being gone. I tried to focus on the shadows dancing across the ceiling and walls cloaked in pale moonlight. It was early in the morning, everyone had fallen asleep long ago, and I lay wide awake. It was like the same night was replaying repeatedly, since nearly all of the nights after we returned had been spent like this. If on the off chance I was able to doze off, Damon filled my thoughts and haunted my dreams, keeping me restless.

I clenched my eyes closed as my shoulders began to shake with heavy, silent sobs. Enough of my mind was aware to be careful not to wake Tristan, who was dozing lightly in a chair on the far vaulted wall. Even though he acted strong for me, the way his sword was rested against the old rocking chair, showed that even he had nightmares.

Wiping my constant tears on the soft bedspread, I flipped to my side and let the grips of exhaustion take my mind.

While darkness was all that encased my mind, it was comforting, at least until the voices began to scream again.

"Free us! Free us!" They chanted, their voices gripping at the walls of my mind.

"No! Leave me alone!" I tried to run, but they followed me everywhere.

Every night of lost sleep and every waking hour.

Before the voices could begin again, a sharp pain came over me, pulling me from this fragmenting reality.

I jumped up in the bed, gasping for air, my face coated with sweat that was slowly mixing with the tears pouring from my eyes.

This time, I had not been silent.

"Sorry, Journey, but you started to scream again." Tristan's concerned lime eyes focused on me with an apologetic stare.

I couldn't meet his eyes. If I did, I would just cry more. Though at this point, I thought the tears would have run out, but they never failed to keep coming. As the loyal friends I did not deserve, Tristan and Piper had been caring for me, but even they knew there was only so much you could do to heal grief.

"Journey?" Piper's small voice called.

I raised my eyes to look at her, even though she was unrecognizable.

She was no longer the bright, young elf I remembered from before the war. Most of her sunken face was covered by thinning blonde hair, which was cut short at the shoulder, becoming more faded by the day. She seemed to be an emaciated shell of the Piper I knew, almost like she would blow away with the slightest gust of breeze. After two weeks, I had stayed the same, but she had only gotten worse.

"Journey?" Her tone was soft before giving out towards the end of my name.

Finally, I met her dull forest eyes and took a painful swallow, my throat burning, "Y-Ye... Yes?" I coughed out.

A concentrated frown created lines in her pale skin as she placed her frail, bony hand on mine, "Was it about Damon again?" She inquired, like every other morning.

Lying, I nodded my head. Not wanting to worry her further.

She offered a small smile and patted my hand before hoisting herself out of the chair. Making her way to the door, she leaned heavily on the chest of drawers and then kept her hand on the walls as she shuffled down the hall. She disappeared behind a pale green wall covered in growing ivy that seemed to be sprouting as spring was approaching the region.

I sighed but was interrupted by a fit of violent coughing.

"Here." Tristan handed me a glass of water. I nodded my thanks as he helped me steady the cup in my trembling hands.

When I finished, I reached to set it on the old chest of drawers beside the bed, dripping some on the ground as I could not stop my hands from shaking.

Tristan lounged back in the tired armchair as I pulled myself out of bed, letting one of Piper's nightgowns flow around my ankles. I leaned on the bedpost at the foot of the bed, and shakily crossed to the desk which sat beneath the large window. As I slowly regained my strength, I threw back the shear curtain and sighed.

Sunrise...

"Are you still well enough for training today?" Tristan's voice was low.

I pried myself from the window and leaned against the desk, like every other surface in Piper's cottage it was cluttered with books and overgrown plants. Holding my hand out in front of me, I imagined a gold stream of liquid flowing through the veins visible through my pink skin. As I imagined it, gold particles began to splatter down my arm and hand, igniting the magic within me. Heat began to simmer on my skin, and I pulled in the magic before the power became unbearable.

"I'll take that as a yes." Tristan crossed the room and took my hand, examining it closely, "No burning this time. You are slowly getting better at controlling it."

I offered a smile, knowing he could see through it, like I could see through the clear window.

Turning back to the window, a wave of sadness washed over me. I had a perfect view of the pale orange sky mixing with the pink clouds that seemed to be painted by the most delicate hand of a painter, like somebody was making a perfect masterpiece of purpose.

"Journey…" Tristan's voice was nothing but a whisper from behind me, "I know you miss him."

Tears threatening to spill onto my cheeks, I turned to him.

His warm, dark hair had gone uncut for much longer than needed, and covered much of his face, but his lime eyes still shone through the dark layers. After being frustrated countless times with me, he was fighting over the control of the beast living in his blood. After everything we had been through, I was grateful to still have him by my side, but knew it was not fair to him.

He cleared his throat, "I really hate to remind you… but… well, Journey." He sighed, placing his hands on my shoulders and meeting my eyes, "H-He isn't coming back. A-And… I think it is time you begin to move past this." Knowing how it affected my mind in the past, I could tell it was hard for him to say.

Before I could respond a loud crash sounded downstairs, followed by a harsh yell from Piper.

Tristan was rushing out of the door in one quick stride.

'Damon isn't coming back…' So why does it still feel like he is here with me.

I stared out of the window, almost being able to see Damon standing with me, his lapis eyes sparkling with laughter and a kind smile tugging at his lips. The thought made a single tear slip down my cheek. I hated the memories, but at the same time I would not want to forget them. A sharp pain ripped through my chest, not in sorrow, but more so in frustration. I was frustrated that it felt as though he was standing right there with me, like I could just reach out and pull him into my arms. To me, he was still there when everyone else said he was gone. He would have called it hope that I carried with me. Hope that he was still alive. But hope would not bring him back.

It seems more like cruel and unusual punishment rather than hope. If only I could have prevented it.

The Heavens know if there was any way I could have stopped this, I would have.

"But you didn't." The voice that remained in my head stated harshly, *"You knew what he would do, how he felt about you, and yet you let him sacrifice himself. All so you could live a life you don't deserve to live. What a weak excuse for a symbol of strength and protection. What would anyone ever see in you?"*

I shook the thoughts away, though I could still feel them lingering in the back of my mind. Running my fingers through my tangled mass of hair, I pulled it over my shoulder and twisted it into a messy braid. Pausing for a second to admire the cuff bracelet adorning my wrist.

The worn leather stretched around my thinning wrist, expanding into a circle towards the center, where a leafless tree was etched in black. Various markings were etched in black along the band, and when it caught the sun just right, you could see the small specks of gold in the leather. It was a gift from my grandmother, along with a journal that only appeared when we escaped Althea's Realm.

I looked to the desk where the journal sat peacefully basking in the sun. A bad feeling came over me as I ran my hand over the embossed tree on the cover. The magic in the pit of my stomach began aching to be released. It called to me, beckoning me to read the secrets which were written between its hand-pressed pages.

"Journey." Tristan calling my name pulled my mind from whatever trance the Journal had over me.

I snatched my hand away and spun on my heals to Tristan standing in the old doorway.

He placed a pail of water on the old wooden floor and handed me a small vial of clear liquid that glowed when I touched it.

"Soothing Serum. It will heal your throat so you can at least speak without pain."

"P-Piper?" My voice was hoarse and strained from the countless screams that resulted from the nightmares.

He let out a small chuckle, offering his charismatic smirk, "I put her back to bed. Between the two of you I'll never get another night of beauty sleep." He teased as I let out a small, shaky laugh.

Tristan cleared his throat, stopping the moment short and returning to a less appealing serious tone, "It's still early. You could go for a walk… clear your head."

I nodded and drank the cool liquid after he exited the room, closing the door behind him.

Placing the empty vial on the cluttered chest, I took the cloth from the handle of the wooden pail and wiped my face clean with the freezing water. I caught a glimpse of myself in the water.

The distorted image of myself reflected the way I felt inside. My figure, once full and healthy, was slowly starting to thin with the constant training and lack of sleep. A pair of murky eyes stared back at me, and they seemed almost hollow as I looked deep into them, but they were far from the once brilliant emerald eyes that captured Damon's interest.

"*If only he could see you now…*" *The voice returned,* "*An unwanted leader, an abandoned prophecy, and unworthy of the sacrifices that have been given for you.*"

Taking a deep breath, I swallowed the lump in my throat and took one last look in the water.

You said I was special… but oh how wrong you were.

~ ~ ~

There was a single road that separated Secret Hollow and the new town built on its soil. The kingdom I called home was still repairing from the war that started twelve years ago and ended three years ago. On the other side of the kingdom, where the forest and edge of town once sat was now covered in towering buildings and houses with cobbled streets winding between them. Queen Eslanda came during the aftermath of the war and took over a kingdom that was tired of fighting against people. She used them in their time of need. Not only that, but she completely ignored rebuilding what Secret Hollow was known for, its rich heritage and historical town which had not changed since the Mystics reigned over it. The Queen prided herself on the thought of being able to demolish it one day. Now, with me around, she feared she would never see that day.

The old town was broken and destroyed, nearly stripped of its spirit. What little had been rebuilt held the hearts of the people who remained there. They refused to give up their home, a notion I could easily agree with.

A heavy shoulder slammed against mine. I stumbled but steadied myself before I could fall.

I felt a gloved hand on my shoulder and met the eyes of a guard who was trying to steady me.

"Oh! My apologies, M'Lady." The guard removed his hand and gave a small bow.

'M'Lady'… it had been so long…

"T-That's alright." I stuttered before running off, shielding my head further with my hood, tears threatening to stream from my cold, dry eyes.

My watery vision led me through the broken down town. Then the air changed, and a feeling of calm and peace washed over me, making me stop in my tracks.

An eruption of pink leaves clouded above me, being held by a swirling dark trunk. The tree mesmerized me and called to me, pulling me with a force greater than any other.

I followed the crumbling steps that spiraled around the hill up to the soft grass. Healing my tainted lungs, a deep breath filled my lungs with the swirling mix of magic and wooded air.

The magic pulsing through my veins, I laid my hand on the mighty trunk and smiled. Sitting against the trunk, my head leaned heavily against it, my mind and body finally relaxing.

"Look who we have here." A disembodied voice spoke.

I knew I did not need to, but I peeked over the tall grass to spot Asmund climbing the twisting stairs.

"I thought you could not venture into the town?" I teased.

His charismatic grin appeared, "Please, that was years ago…" He took a seat beside me, his tone becoming serious, "They've forgotten all about me and the kingdom I come from, just like how they've forgotten all about the Mystics and the truth beneath this aching kingdom…"

I met his eyes, but quickly looked away, as I could not face him when he asked the question which he asked every day since we returned:

"What if we showed them the journal, tell them the stories?"

"No." I cut him off, "If the townspeople were to read what is written in that journal… or anyone really, they would surely kill us all."

"Why won't you tell me what is in it?" He searched my face until I met his curious gaze.

I stayed silent before looking away again.

He heaved a sigh, "Alright, I trust you."

The breeze blew through my stray hairs, causing a chill to run down my spine, and a yawn to escape my lips.

"Sleep, nothing can get you here." His voice was low and quiet, nearly lulling me to sleep with every word.

"Don't leave me alone…" I mumbled, half asleep and unaware of what I was saying.

"As long as I am here, you will never be alone." The words were nothing but a whisper against my head.

Nodding, I rested my head against his broad shoulder and dozed lightly.

I tried to relax, but I couldn't. Any thoughts of the journal kept my peace away.

The Mystics' Journal was filled with true stories of the Mystics. Not those fabricated by their scholars. The journal told of the dark truth, and if anyone read it, they would easily realize, these heroes were far from angels.

~2~

INTO THE LIGHT I must go, for my heart no longer beats for this world. I am nothing more than magic with no soul, as it has been stolen from my grasp.

I am sorry, Dear Friend, for we came together and now I must leave alone. I regret that I have forced you to stay and to wait for her, but she must be guided properly and taught how to understand our past and our purpose. By the time you return to our world, I will have moved on in my years. Perhaps I will remember you, though your life will only be beginning, and mine... I hope mine will barely be ending.

It is time that I leave, that I move on from this world. I will retreat to my realm, and there I will take my relic.

You will never get to see it, but this place I have created is beautiful. I made it beautiful for him. I have also forged this journal with my magic. If I did so correctly, it should recreate our story. I know you warned me about this, because I once believed no one deserved to go through what I and every other group of Mystics have gone through, but I can't bring myself to let him be forgotten again. Until she arrives, my relic will hide the journal and protect it from getting into the wrong hands. Our story must never be revealed... if the people were to find out what we have done, and how we remember our regrets, I truly believe they will try to destroy the Mystics. You must never let this happen, and you must tell her to protect the journal with her life.

The time has come that I take my relic and let the new generation of Mystics take their stand. So, here in this beautiful resting place is where two lovers, punished by the world, will lay to rest together. Because of my magic, it will be safe. The air will be full of healing until the magic leaves. This is the place where two souls come together again... and maybe because of me, it will stay like this forever.

Goodbye, Dear Friend.

~ ~ ~

Damon's POV:

Blood had seeped through my shirt and coated my hand in the hot red liquid. Any trace of magic in the air had dissipated, leaving me feeling only the dark magic flooding off of Calvin.

Calvin...

Even the name in my head stirred my anger. He was the reason I was in this mess. The reason she couldn't live a normal life. I would be by her side now if it wasn't for him.

As the blood that remained in my body began to boil, the pounding in my head pulsed louder.

Soon the darkness started to enclose my vision, and I welcomed it until a hard hit to my boot sent a shooting pain through my wound and made me jump, causing only more pain.

"Are you still alive?" Calvin's disgusting voice came over me.

"No." I responded in hopes he would leave me to rest.

He chuckled, "I do wonder how much time has passed in the other realm. Probably not much… for your sake at least."

Saying nothing, I only grunted.

"It might just be rewarding for me to say… it was only the wishful thinking in your soul to think they would come back for you."

After coughing violently, blood seeping into the corners of my mouth, I stuttered, "I-It's call… called- It's hope." I coughed again, the taste of blood becoming over-whelming, "I-I hope the… they don't- co…back."

His icy eyes went wide under his black tufts of hair, and a drop of sweat dripped off the side of his pale face.

The darkness started to spread across my eyes again, making the pain subside.

I only hope she has found happiness without me.

~3~

"HAND'S UP, JOURNEY." Milku's voice carried across the empty field.

I lifted my sore, aching arms again, blocking each of Milku's gem-tipped arrows with a wall of magic energy. She purposely aimed them in blind spots and holes in my magic, making sure my reflexes were still sharp. Finally, after a few dozen arrows, Milku held her hand up and motioned for a break.

Tired and covered in sweat despite the cool air, I shuffled over to where Tristan and Asmund lounged under the shade of the few trees nearby. Much of the field at the base of the Mystics' Tree had been cleared of crops and debris. It made a good spot for training, as it was flat and still close enough to the Mystics' Tree to replenish magic easily. The boys also liked it, considering it had a few rocks shaded by the trees that they enjoyed resting on when they took a moment to be here. The only downfall was its proximity to the separating road, which made the new townspeople anxious.

Falling against the surface of the cool rock, I took a moment to catch my breath. This was an off-chance day that Tristan was here, as it was usually just Asmund. Tristan patted my shoulder and offered a smile before leaving to talk to Milku.

"You're getting better. And doing so quickly." Asmund's small compliment was enough to lift my broken spirits.

Habitually, I pulled my honey brown hair out of its confines and began to redo the tangled braid behind my head. After pulling it over my shoulder to finish the last few strands, I caught Asmund watching me, a small smile shining in his black eyes.

Before I could say anything, Milku's voice ordered me back to the center of the field.

Hesitantly, I stood and crossed to her, keeping my guard up as she had been known to throw an attack when I least expected it.

A breeze shifted through the branches of the pink tree, making the hair on my arms stand up. Spinning around, I threw my arms up blocking my face, my magic unconsciously created a wall of liquid gold around me. The wall penetrated a spell of magic from Tristan and two gemmed arrows from Milku.

"Nice reflexes, Journey!" Milku called from a few yards away, "Let's see how fast you can react." I could barely hear her voice because of the whipping wind.

With divine speed she aimed three arrows and shot them from the bow that usually cloaked her back, striking against her iridescent hair.

I prepared myself for attacks on both sides and rolled to the left, letting both attacks collide with each other. I spun and blocked another arrow from Milku, which came too close for comfort. Before I could even aim, I shot a blast of magic to destroy Tristan's attack. However, I missed Tristan's attack and quickly ducked, letting it fly over my head where it was stopped by Milku.

As I rose, I paused for a second to catch my breath and calm my pounding heartbeat. A sense of magic came over my left side, pushing me over and throwing a spell to destroy an attack from Milku, who had moved significantly closer. I quickly went through a mental check list about close-range attacks.

Without thought, they both stopped, but Milku had failed to call hold. My guess was they both had spoken about this to throw me off.

I stood still, my magic on edge, begging to be freed from the anticipation.

"How many times must I tell you, this is not a training ground!" A shrill voice pierced the air across the field.

Without warning the magic within me surfaced, being held at bay for too long. The more I tried to bring it in, the more uncontrollable it became. Before I could scream a surge of energy came rushing through my veins, and made waves of magic tower around me, and then fall to the ground at my feet. With my magic strength growing and constant training, we had learned if I tried hard enough, I could control the liquid magic that seeped into the soil from the Mystics' Tree. We knew this posed a large threat to the people and us, so we tried to avoid it at all cost, but when my magic took control, there was nothing I could do to stop it.

For a moment, everything stopped and we thought it was over. That was before the guards rushed us.

Fear froze me to the ground as I looked from the guards to Queen Eslanda. Without any permission from me, I felt my magic rise from the pit of my stomach, and adrenaline rush through my veins. A powerful aura pushed through my body, destroying every barrier I built. This resulted in an amount of energy that not only could I not control, but stronger than anyone could stop.

Around me, thousands of people appeared, facing the guards. They created a sea of gray, nearly translucent people. Some of them charged the guards throwing their weapons to the ground, which did not seem to hurt the people. After detaining the guards, they turned to me and began running.

Their voices were those that haunted me each day, "Free us!" They all screamed over each other.

I fought to control the magic that sent them, but it was not under my control. I began pushing them away, kicking them from grabbing my feet as everyone stood helplessly.

More began to swarm towards me, yelling over each other with the same words, which echoed through my mind. The others around me began to scream my name, trying desperately to help.

I summoned a dome of magic around me, to at least keep the people away, and covered my ears still being able to hear their voices.

"Journey..." A familiar voice hummed.

I opened my eyes to see the woman walking gracefully towards me, a sad smile adorning her pale face, cloaked in long white hair. I recognized her from my conversation before the war.

"Just close your eyes and breath, Journey. Do not let their voices overwhelm you." She spoke in my head, rather than from around me.

I followed her instructions and focused on her voice only, letting the others slowly fade.

"Open your eyes, Journey. See what you have made true." Her familiar words faded as I hesitantly opened my eyes.

The people had vanished, leaving me only with Tristan, Milku, and Asmund. The Queen and her guards were nowhere to be found.

I looked to Milku and Tristan, who had each frozen.

"You cannot hide yourself anymore. They know of the danger you possess and fear you because of it." The constant voice in my head pressed further.

Their stares were piercing me, causing my body to erupt in violent shaking, and I wanted nothing more than to escape this world.

Looking to Asmund, I expected him to give me a calm smile, his eyes speaking to me, telling me it would be alright. But instead they did not invite me to get lost in the endless darkness. As I looked deeper, I saw something I had never seen appear in his black eyes.

Fear.

~ ~ ~

Tristan's POV:

The narrow streets that filed between the tall buildings of Secret Hollow made it feel more like a kingdom than the previous quaint village. I still had not decided whether I liked the new kingdom or the old village better. The old village reminded me of home, but it also reminded me of my mother. The kingdom reminded me that I was a beast, one that was not accepted by society, but it did not bring the dread of thinking of my home village.

Peering around the side of my hunter green hood, I watched Milku closely. Her squinted eyes held a piercing glare, and she seemed to be lost in thought.

We continued through the heart of the kingdom like this for some time, before Milku's stern voice caused me to jump out of my thoughts, "With time she should learn to control it. Even with the magic's strength, it has to be controlled somehow. Though I fear with her amount of stress, that that time could be longer than the next time she loses control." She paused and glanced over to me, meeting my eyes before I could steal my glance away.

"You know it is rude to stare." She commented as I quickly looked away, but did not mention it further as she continued speaking, "Tell me, Brother, how is Journey adjusting to Secret Hollow?"

I swallowed, "Secret Hollow was her home, and now she feels lost without it."

"It seems as though the result of the war was as hard on her as it was on us." Her eyes wandered away before continuing, "After Lady Ashton retook her throne, chaos had already ensued. It took years for everyone to finally stop fighting. And after it did, we returned to a broken, nearly unrepairable version of Secret Hollow."

She sighed, "We almost didn't continue on after we lost all of you. Journey brought these people a hope for a better future, and without her, their hope was slowly diminishing. Even I had to admit without someone there to lead us, to be a light in such a dark time, it seemed so much easier to move on from this place and find another kingdom to call home…. When Queen Eslanda came, we were forced to build a new kingdom, covering the scars and history of the war. We were too tired of fighting to do so against her. At the time we merely thought we were only re-building Secret Hollow, but we later realized we were building New Hollow.

"During the war, people were pushed to become heroes when they were only children, and then they were treated like servants when they returned home. Magic was slowly made to be only an aspect of power and used for the Queen's benefit. Yet, through everything we were put through, our greatest agony was losing all of you."

I watched her careful, even though she refused to look at me. For whatever reason as we walked and she spilled the pain she had been keeping locked up for twelve years, she reminded me so much of our mother in her final years.

Her lime eyes, which our mother had gifted the both of us, met mine as she choked back tears, "That time was difficult on me, as it was on everyone. It reminded me of when Mother left, when Father learned of my magic and its power. The confines of these walls felt like the confines of the orphanage he sent me to. That orphanage was the place where people abandoned magic users to the elders. To them we were freaks meant to destroy the rightful workings of society. Beasts, those labeled as witches, even the occasional Metronite was confined within those four walls hidden from the rest of the world. The only difference I can discern between the two is that here, at least my magic is accepted…" Her voice trailed off as I nodded and offered a small smile.

Ahead of us, a group of guards gathered outside one of the quarters, which housed the guards that were not married.

"Isn't that the beast the locals keeping speaking of? The one who returned with the one claiming to be Lady Althea. Remember, they claim to have come from Althea's Realm, which we all know is hogwash." A scrawny guard rambled, more than likely new to the guard force and trying to fit in. I knew the type all too well.

Another recruit stuttered, "S-Shouldn't… Shouldn't we have repr…reprimanded him by now. He is dangerous to have among the townspeople."

Milku's temper flared as she shoved past me, her hands glowing white with her magic.

"Watch what you speak of my Brother," she spat at the group.

"Or what, White Witch?" The leader assigned over the group, pushed forward, a cocky smirk covering his face.

Though he intended the name to scare her, Milku took pride in the strength of her magic. It came with our lineage, and we were taught to never be ashamed of being related to Emerson the Peacekeeper.

"You will learn just why I was given that name," she muttered.

His stony eyes squinted, competing with her piercing glare, "If you use your magic to harm me, you will be thrown in prison. Or have you forgotten that your magic is to only be used for the Queen?"

"I will use my magic however I please." Scowling, she stomped towards me, but not before slyly summoning a small gemstone at his feet, making them all jump backwards, fear drawing them away.

"Don't listen to them, Tristan. Everyone that matters knows you would never hurt anyone."

I nodded but could not push out the sound of their voices behind us.

"Why would she defend him?" One recruit asked.

I heard him break the crystal to small shards, and spit into a pot that sat outside of the quarters, "Because that man is a coward."

'A coward'...

~4~

ASMUND WAS FOLLOWING closely behind me as I navigated our way through the streets of Secret Hollow, or as the new townspeople called it, New Hollow. It seemed everything had changed, like my home had been taken and replaced with an empty shell of what it once was. Being surrounded by so many people, but not knowing any of them made me think back to the time August had taken me to Evnock.

August...

It wasn't long ago when I last saw the temperamental Dark Soldier, but I knew he would've changed more than I could ever imagine. Besides being promoted to Captain of New Hollow's guard, he must have taken our disappearance hard, especially Damon's.

As his name popped into my head, I stopped and lifted my eyes from the newly cobbled streets. Before me sat a busy marketplace with stalls around selling various items. Attached to the far side, barely seen under a welcoming arch which connected the two mountains on either side, were multiple docks hanging over the now tainted water. It was obnoxiously loud and over-crowded with both people and livestock filling the open area.

A dreadful feeling sunk in my chest realizing the white sand beach was no more and the swaying ships blocked the fading sun.

For a moment, just the slightest moment, I thought of how I was glad Damon had not returned with us. The place each of us once called home was tainted… and it was not our home anymore.

'It is the best place to watch the sunset… I wanted to show you that the world is full of beautiful colors that you are missing.' I could still picture his lapis eyes as they sparkled that night.

"Keep moving, Lady!" A man with a thick accent shoved past us.

Jumping away from my deep thoughts, I pressed forward into the craziness of the surrounding market stalls.

Asmund did not speak as he followed me, keeping his head down and thoughts silent.

The setting sun glistened from a stall a few feet away, bouncing off the blade of a sword that hung on the wall, grabbing my attention.

A white steel sword hung on the back wall between various misshapen weapons. It was scuffed and the leather wrapped handle was darkened with stains. The small gemstone pressed at the top, given to me by Milku to one day be able to pass my magic through the sword, needed polishing, but there was no mistaking it. I didn't think I would ever see it after leaving it in the forest when I went to face Calvin.

"How much?" I nodded to the sword, remembering the day Ozara had gifted it to me.

The gentleman was older, hunched over with wrinkles covering his face. He looked up at me with squinted eyes and smiled, "It will be a bit pricey. You see, it was once wielded by Lady Althea herself."

"Oh, come now, Cecil! Don't you recognize her!" A deep voice hollered over the crowd.

Before I could see who the familiar voice belonged to, August's cognac eyes met mine as he slung his arm over my shoulder, pushing Asmund away.

"This is Lady Althea herself!"

The market went silent at August's overly loud comment.

Cecil looked at August with suspicion.

"Oh fine! You drive a hard bargain, Cecil, but your prices are the fairest!" He placed some smashed coins on the counter and held his hand out for the sword.

The man counted the silver pieces, nodded at August, and handed him the sword.

Being led by August, who nodded to many of the people as we passed, we pushed our way back through the crowd to a small side street off the docks.

"Your sword." August held the guard of the sword, carefully allowing me to grasp the handle.

I ran my finger along the flat of the blade, stealing a line of dust and grime as I did. It felt strange holding it again.

Slipping the sword into my empty scabbard, I reached up and wrapped my arms around August's broad shoulders.

He had grown taller as he matured. Since being promoted to Captain of the guard he had gotten significantly more muscular. His wavy brown hair was allowed to grow down to his shoulders. As he left my embrace, I noticed the red ring that once surrounded the pupil of his cognac eyes, was no longer visible. He seemed different, happier. His posture was filled with pride and strength. This was the place he dreamed of, the way he always envisioned Secret Hollow.

"There you are!" A small voice approached from behind me.

Two women and a young man walked around us and stood beside August.

One of the women seemed familiar, when she lifted her ice eyes to meet mine, a smile caught her lip.

The not-so-young Metronite practically ran and wrapped her arms around me. She was still the same height as me, maybe a tad taller. Her straight, white hair contrasted against her dark brown skin that was adorned with freckles. Her face was painted with white paint on her cheeks and chin, as well as a crescent moon on her forehead. It was usually saved for Metronites of high ranking in tribes, but Basil used it to accentuate the guard emblem that was placed on her chest. I did not see the emblem at first, as it was covered with multiple layers, giving her curvy body even more volume, but she wore the pride without needing the emblem.

"Basil, I can't believe it! You're all grown up!" I smiled as she pulled away.

Her big smile never left her face, "That's right! Second in Command now."

The young man took a step beside Basil and held his hand out, "Kova, Senior Scout of New Hollow's Guard Force."

I placed my hand in his and stole a glimpse of him as he bowed. He wasn't the most recognizable Metronite. He was tall and rather scrawny for being in the guard. His oily, black hair covered his pale face, making him the opposite of Basil, though they both shared a face of freckles. It was hard to believe he was nearly twenty, as I vividly remembered the day, we rescued him from the streets of Tuhe. I also remembered that he was considered a heterochromia wolf. His eyes, one brown and one blue, shone with youth, though his deep voice revealed his maturity.

Standing beside each other, you would not think they were siblings, even if only being adopted siblings. Basil favored her mother's features and embraced the culture from the North Metronite tribe and Kova was very prominently with the Southern tribe features.

"There is no need to be so formal, Kova. Lady Journey was there when we found you."

Kova looked at his sister and then back at me, a goofy smile coming to his face, "How would I know? I was only a lad then." He had the slightest hint of an accent.

Basil stood on her toes, barely reaching Kova's shoulder, and ruffled his hair, "Hardly even that, Pup."

I smiled at the scene, knowing Kova filled a hole left in Basil's heart after her brother, Zephyr, was pronounced dead. The time was hard on Basil and her mother, Lyra, but Kova brought the missing link they needed to feel whole again.

After a moment of catching up with Basil and Kova, hearing that Lyra had stayed in Tuhe after the war, I looked over to August who had linked arms with the other woman.

Watching curiously, I forgot it would eventually count as staring.

August cleared his throat, ushering a silence out of the two Metronites, "Journey... I would like you to meet Celeste... my wife."

"Oh, stop acting like you are flustered." She smiled.

The woman was nearly as tall as him but was curvy in appearance as her long purple dress hugged her curves. Her dark tan skin glistened in the dusk rays of the sun like bronze.

"It is a pleasure to meet you." Vibrant orange curls bounced around her shoulders, her warm brown eyes meeting mine, "August has told me many great things about you."

Once I finished staring at the beautiful girl, I couldn't help but laugh, "I never thought I would hear of August speaking well of me."

A teasing glare entered August's eyes, reminding me of his true personality hidden beneath the Dark Soldier's surface, "Please, I would speak well about you anytime someone asked... And even if I didn't, it is bad luck to speak ill of the dead."

As the sun began to sink further beneath the horizon, the market slowly started to die down.

Finally, in a private moment, August spoke up and asked the one question I was dreading, "S..So Journey… I just have to ask… I ha… I have to know…" He paused, gathering himself before continuing, "What exactly happened to Damon? When do you plan on opening the portal and bringing him home?" You could hear his voice choking back tears.

"Calvin… Calvin took control of him before we left this world. He turned his memories of me, of all of us," I motioned to everyone, "When we were taken to Althea's Realm, Calvin tried to absorb Althea's relic, but the relic chose me instead."

"You found Althea's relic?" Basil cut in.

I nodded, "It was what healed Damon of the spell Calvin cast over him. Calvin grew furious and tried to kill Damon, which I was able to stop. That was when the light appeared."

"It must have been when Piper opened the portal. She had been trying to do that for years." Celeste's small comment was barely heard from beside August.

I continued, "I was protecting Damon, trying to convince Calvin to let him go back. I told him I was willing to stay if he would let Damon return to this world. But… But Damon grabbed me and pushed me away into the portal. T-Then he took Calvin's attack for me… The portal closed before I could do anything."

"But you can open it." August had the slightest sliver of hope as he spoke.

I looked away, unwilling to take away the one thing he had left, the one thing we all had left of him. The hope of his return.

"I don't understand, they said you could open the portal." Disbelief lingered in his voice.

I tried to explain myself, "Even if I opened the portal, Damon is more than likely-"

"Do you not care to bring him back?" The red ring in his eyes expanded as he took a step towards me, Celeste grasping at his hand.

Asmund stepped in front of me, his hand stationary at the hilt of his sword.

"You were supposed to die, not him!" He yelled, took another step, and yanked his hand from Celeste's.

Asmund quickly put himself between me and August.

"There is no need for this situation to escalate." Asmund's tone was calm, yet his stance was threatening.

August began to have a disgusted look in his eyes, as he looked Asmund up and down, thinking he could take him if he wanted, "Who do you think you are, forcing your way into this matter?"

"Between the magic that you possess, and the magic that Journey has yet to learn to control, I am not forcing myself into the situation, but saving countless lives from being injured or ended." He lifted his eyes to meet August's.

"August, stop this." Celeste called to him, but he ignored her.

As August's temper rose higher, my magic began to bubble in the pit of my stomach.

I tried to call the magic off, knowing that if I used it, the voices would be able to find me again.

"Journey!" August called while being semi held back by Kova and Basil.

The magic had already begun to surface and the only thing I could do to stop it, was to aim it at the ground. This resulted in deep holes burned into the cobbled streets, which I allowed to continue until the magic was depleted enough to be controlled. The people who remained in the marketplace slowly started to leave, trying not to panic.

Once the magic was controlled, a sharp pain lifted up my arms, and the cool air made them sting.

Asmund came to me as I winced in pain, "Are you alright?" He grabbed my hands in his and studied them.

The pain became excruciating at that point, and I glanced down at my hands, feeling nauseous as I did.

My hands and part way up my wrists had been burnt black from the magic. They were not bleeding, but every gust of breeze made them feel as though they were being burned all over again.

Asmund's voice became concerned as he looked between my hands and the marketplace, not caring that his hands were also being burnt from the magic residue on mine, "Medic!" He yelled, hoping someone would come to our need.

My vision began to get hazy and the depletion of magic made my head spin. Asmund, taking careful notice, moved to allow me to lean heavily on his shoulder.

Celeste pushed between Basil and Kova, taking my hands from Asmund, "We need to get you to the medic station."

She guided me along, making sure I was strong enough to keep upright by myself.

"Journey! Journey, why won't you bring him back?" Pain seared August's voice.

In my hazed state there was no filter to his feelings or mine.

"B-Because…" I stopped, turned, and met his eyes, tears threatening to fall on my cheeks, "He's… He's gone."

~ ~ ~

Asmund's POV:

The tunnel had been carved as a passageway through the mountain. According to Journey, it had once been used as Secret Hollow's marketplace, with small dugouts off to the side to act as archives. But that was long ago, now the place had been recovered as a medic station.

Celeste finished wrapping Journey's hands, before standing back and admiring the bandage work.

Journey had not met my eyes, but to be fair, I had not met hers either. I couldn't shake the fearful feeling in the back of my mind. The feeling of a knowledge I was not supposed to know.

Across the room, Piper was sitting with her head in her hands. I did not know the elf well, but I noticed she kept getting in worse condition as the days continued. Journey was also worried about her, though she tried not to show it.

"I have to apologize once more for August's temper." Celeste spoke up in the otherwise silent room.

"Celeste, I have told you to stop that. August is a grown man. He can apologize for his own mistakes; you are not the one responsible for his choices." Piper snapped, which seemed unusual for the peaceful looking elf.

"Do you need some chamomile for your head?" Celeste inquired, ignoring the comment.

Piper nodded, "Something stronger if we have it."

Celeste nodded and hurried out of the old archive.

"I still find it hard to believe August is married. Especially to a girl as sweet as Celeste." Journey finally spoke.

"As do I, and I attended the wedding." Piper pushed her head back.

"Honestly, when she arrived here, August was a mess. A complete drunk who drowned the loss of his fallen brother in ale. It was a wonder she could get through to him, but she has a need to help everyone. Sometimes I think that girl is too nice to him."

Journey nodded, "They just seem so different. He has this powerful aura around him, and she is… doesn't."

"Are you serious?" Piper asked, seeming annoyed.

"What do you mean?" Journey truly had no reasoning to the difference between the couple.

I let out a soft chuckle, "What she means is that you are terrible at being a magic user. Your thoughts of them are not of them but of their magic. It is not that Celeste is not powerful. You only think that of her because you are comparing her to someone who has magic while she has no magic."

"She is human?" Journey seemed astonished.

Piper sighed, "Magic users have slowly begun to die out after the war. With so few people believing we make a true difference to this world magic has slowly begun to diminish."

Celeste appeared before Journey could say anything. She left with Piper leaning heavily on her shoulder, tossing a small smile back to us.

Journey rose and crossed to the windowsill and clenched her fist, watching as the bandage tightened around her hand. She then crossed to a bookshelf and began searching books left out by Piper.

I peered over her shoulder and read a small passage about opening the portal.

"What are you thinking of?" I finally inquired.

"If magic users are disappearing, and we don't have time to find the other Mystics, this is the only way to open the portal."

"You are not putting yourself in danger for this again."

She sighed and slammed the book close, "That is not your choice to make."

I finally lifted my eyes up and met hers, "Tell me what is wrong, Journey. You have been hiding it from everyone else," I paused and took her bandaged hand, "But you don't have to hide it from me."

She snatched her hand and paced to the other side of the room, gently dropping the book on top of a pile, "I...I can't."

"I told you, as long as I am here, you have no reason to be alone. Whatever you are going through, we are going through together. Whether you like it or not, I've got your back."

"I just don't want you to think less of me. I am human, I always have been, at heart at least. I will make mistakes... I have made mistakes..." She trailed off for a moment, "I'm not neglecting my people, but Damon is important to me. And yes, my loyalty lies with my people, but these people don't want me anymore."

"No one is questioning your loyalty to your people." I stated, trying to make my point known.

"Yet I am the one who is keeping secrets from them!" Anger burned in her voice and she clenched her fists in frustration.

I crossed to her, "The only secrets you are keeping are the ones you have the right to keep."

She shook her head, golden honey hair falling from her braid, "I'm putting us all in danger…"

"What kind of danger?" Suspicion lingered in my voice. I knew she was talking about the journal.

She sighed, "… The stories in the journal… only a few have appeared, but it revealed why Althea created the journal. She did it to recreate her story, to force her descendants to live out the same miserable story as hers. She wanted a way to bring Azguard back, so she forged the journal to make every generation of Mystics follow the same pattern."

"You would do the same thing if you lost someone you-" I caught myself before I finished the sentence.

"No, she sentenced everyone after Azguard to death. Not only that, but she abandoned her people. She was a coward, not the hero everyone saw her as."

There was a small moment of silence between us.

"She did not want her magic; she saw it as only a bond she couldn't break out of. While I can't control my magic, I still think of it as a gift instead of a burden. The only thing binding me is the fear these people have of me."

"What do you mean?" My eyes darted to her.

She fiddled with the bracelet on her wrist and cleared her throat, "They are afraid of my magic… and you are too. I saw the look you gave me in the field today."

"I-I"

"Save it. I'm used to it by now. I'm a danger to people, they have the right to be fearful," She looked up at me, though I refused to catch her stare, "Even you."

I sighed, adding a small chuckle to it, "No matter how powerful your magic becomes, I will not be fearful of you. Between all the times we fought, I won the most remember… the look you saw in the field was not fear of you, but rather fear of what I discovered about your magic."

She inquired, "M-My... magic?"

"I realized today what type of magic you possess."

"Why would you not tell me?" A hint of excitement sparkled in her emerald eyes.

"Because I know my relic will automatically be the opposite and I don't want to come to grips with it. Unlike your magic, mine is actually dangerous."

I slumped against the bookcase, burying my head in my hands before pushing my fingers through my growing black hair. How immature we must have sounded, arguing over who was more dangerous.

"I'm... I'm sorry, Asmund. I didn't think..."

Harsher than I meant, I interrupted her, "No, you didn't. That's the problem."

"Asmund..." Entering the shadows fogging my mind, she crossed over to me, leaving the rays of the sunset, and wrapped her arms around my shoulders.

Knowing they were few and far between, I returned her embrace and savored the moment. As I rested my head on her shoulder, I thought.

She is kind and beautiful even as broken as she feels. Perhaps it is because I know who she once was and am determined to bring her back. I gazed at the book that started this conversation and had somehow turned it into a small argument.

If I don't bring her back to her old self for her sake, then I can at least do it for his sake.

"Journey… this does not make it any easier to tell you about your magic any more than before."

She smiled, a teasing glare entered her eyes, "Fine, you caught me." She laughed.

Allowing a small chuckle, I hugged her tighter, knowing the time would come eventually that I would have to reveal her magic.

"Your magic attracts those who have not yet moved on from this world. You have the ability to see and aid those who have a final regret binding them to this world. Your magic brings life to people who have otherwise died. The people you see are the lost souls doomed to wander this world alone." I whispered.

She pulled away and met my eyes, staring silently for a moment, "But if my magic brings life… then yours…" Her voice was breathless, and tears began to ring in her eyes.

"Brings death."

~5~

"YOU NEED TO focus on the calling inside of you." Basil was face to face with me, telling me to focus, yet my mind kept wandering to Asmund's revelation.

"Are you even listening to me?" Basil paused her lecture, "If you are going to learn to transform, you have to listen and be able to understand what I mean when I say embrace the creature within you."

I shook my thoughts away and tucked them into the back of my mind, "Alright, I'm listening."

"Good." She nodded at Kova.

"Transformation, while it falls into the category of magic, uses no magic at all. The creature you turn into, in your case a wolf, shares the same soul as you. You are one with one another. All you have to do is call on them and allow them to take control of your physical form." Kova explained.

Basil stood a few feet in front of Kova and stayed silent for a moment. Her body then morphed into a large wolf. She shook her head, letting white fur fall to the ground.

She looked up at me with her piercing blue eyes and a wolfish grin.

"Wolves of the same tribe or family can communicate with each other through telepathy. Otherwise it is up to body language to determine what they are saying."

Basil pranced in a circle, her father's creek stone dangling on a large piece of leather around her neck.

"Though it will take a moment to get used to how the animal's body works, the animal's instincts are still with you and will guide you along the way."

I laughed at the goofy grin on Basil's face as she seemed to mimic her little brother, "What now?" I asked.

"It's your turn. Go ahead, call on the wolf inside you."

I glanced down at myself, envisioning a wolf jumping out of me and I encouraged it.

It did not work even though I kept trying to encourage the jumping wolf to come out.

"It's not working!" I yelled, sending a blast of magic into the nearby tree, which made me feel slightly better.

"Remember, Journey, it is not magic. It is something that has to come completely natural." Kova reminded me.

I glanced over at Asmund, who offered a smile before mouthing 'I believe in you.'

I returned the smile, a blush creeping to my cheeks. A gust of wind blew against my flustered face, cooling it from its heat. The leaves of the Mystics' Tree rustled above, and I remembered the feeling of it calling to me.

I closed my eyes and imagined the feeling I got from both the Mystics' Tree and staring into Asmund's dark eyes. I imagined the world melting from around me, every physical thing binding me fell apart in shards. In a way, I was free. In my ears a steady beating rang out. I realized it was my heartbeat, I was finally focusing on what was within me.

A sudden power overtook me, but it was not an uncontrolled power, in fact it was a comfortable force. I let it take over and did not fight against it.

As I opened my eyes, I jumped, hitting the ground with a large thud. I peered down at my feet and smiled at four paws that had slipped from underneath me.

~ ~ ~

Asmund's POV:

A large, golden honey wolf lay where Journey had once stood. Her large emerald eyes blinked at me and a wolfish grin filled with pride covered her face.

She regained her footing and picked up one paw at a time.

The white wolf, clearly from the Northern tribe, trotted a circle around her and bent down into a stalking stance. Journey followed her movement with her eyes, tilting her head when Basil hunched low to the ground.

Before Journey could figure out what Basil was doing, Basil leaped on her and wrestled her to the ground.

I began to laugh harder than I had in a long time at the shocked look frozen on Journey's face.

"Not funny, Asmund..." Her voice popped into my head.

"It really is, Journey." I responded, trying to calm my laughter.

Kova glanced curiously back at me as Basil attempted to help Journey up with her snout.

"You can understand her?" Kova's mismatched eyes went wide.

"Just the same as I normally can."

Basil transformed back into her human form, leaving Journey as a wolf that nearly came to her shoulder.

"It must be like the packs," Basil suggested. "When wolf packs take in new wolves, they can give them the ability to communicate with the rest of the pack. Since you also have a relic, you can communicate with her. It must have been how the Mystics communicated with each other in their spirit forms."

"That is a good observation, Basil," Kova complimented.

Basil smiled, the freckles on her cheeks crinkled into the wrinkles in the corners of her eyes, "Thanks, Pup."

Before the conversation ended, Journey let out a low growl as the wind blew through her brown tufts of hair.

Queen Eslanda marched towards us, her guards on either side. Her black hair was styled in an obnoxious style, and her mint eyes were harsh. She had a mole stamped at the corner of her lip and her whole face seemed stiff as she pointed her nose to the sky. She had been nothing but rude to us since we got back. The others were fortunate to fall under her radar, which seemed to be focused only on Journey.

Journey continued to growl from beside me as the Queen came closer.

"Can no one go for a morning stroll without you-you magic users causing a frenzy?" She shrilled.

Journey ended up losing her hold on the wolf and transformed back into her human form.

"We are not on your side of the kingdom. We have every right to be on Secret Hollow's land." Journey argued.

Understanding the Queen had more authority over them than they cared to admit, Kova and Basil stayed quiet through the argument.

The Queen rolled her eyes, "Please, magic in this kingdom is used solely for my benefit only. Magic users will eventually become extinct, and you doing whatever your doing is not helping it, so stop. The natural order of this world will be restored once you magic users are out of the picture."

Basil and Kova hung their heads, saddened by the thought. I grew angry. Not for the way she was treating Journey, because I knew she could handle the Queen on her own, but because this woman was so inconsiderate of the value of life. She acted as though she did not think of magic users as people.

"My people believe the natural order of this world includes magic. Without magic there would be no hope, imagination, beliefs, child-like joy, or even innocence. If you really want to threaten that society, then I will personally burn this kingdom to the ground to restore the 'natural' order of society." Journey stated with the confidence of her people she had been lacking.

The Queen looked taken aback, "Are you threatening my kingdom?" She squinted her eyes, challenging Journey.

"Yes, I am. Because it was never yours to begin with. You stole it from these people during a time when they had no strength left to fight, but rather wanted to live in peace after nine years of war. Then you go and force them to live in this monstrosity of a kingdom for three years, sucking every bit of hope and joy from them."

The Queen paused.

Journey continued, "The one thing you have yet to learn from your time in Secret Hollow is that we are all family. And you always do *whatever* it takes to protect your family."

~ ~ ~

The door to Piper's cottage slammed shut behind me, and frankly I didn't care. My blood boiled in my veins after my conversation with the Queen. Something about the way she acted entitled to everything made me so furious.

As I hung my gray cloak on the pegs by the front door, I sighed at the messy state of Piper's cottage.

Walking down the hallway that was confined because of the stairway, plants grew overhead and down the walls. After rounding the corner, her beautiful sitting area sat quietly, a fire flickering in the fireplace. The cloth furniture was adorned with blankets thrown about them. Every surface from coffee tables, to windowsills and even the landing to the second floor were cluttered with plants, journals, and various other things Piper had horded over the years. Her dark wood bookcases sagged in the middle under the weight of her massive collection of old books and scrolls, along with other various medicinal mixtures. Enough light shone through the windows to catch the dust floating through the air. The smell of old wood was potent as it mixed with the fumes of the fireplace, making the cottage appeal to at least one sense.

Through the archway to the right of the sitting area, the kitchen sat peacefully. It was a pleasant place which had been filled with early mornings and late night talks you could only have in the dark. A comforting presence came over me as I entered the heart of the cottage.

The back wall was lined with counters on the lower part of the wall, and a large, wood-burning stove took up a portion of the middle. To the wall beside me a small wooden cupboard holding various items sat silently, knowing its place would be there forever. A round table sat in the corner by the back door that led to Piper's garden and forest area.

Piper slaved away over the stove, as she usually did. After seeing me, she smiled and cleared the table of her books and plant clippings she must have been jotting down.

"How was training?" Her voice was soft and almost chipper in tone.

I fell into one of the heavy chairs, which was surprisingly comfortable, "We were interrupted by the Queen again."

Piper laid a hand on my shoulder and cruised from one object to another as she made her way back to the stove, where the makeshift kettle had just whistled.

Piper poured part of the water into a large basin that held some of her clothes before taking a few herbs from the shelf above and breaking them up into the water. She poured the remainder of the water into two cups and plucked two leaves from the overgrown plant on the windowsill.

As she made her way to me, a cup in each hand, she lost her balance and dropped the cups as she reached out to catch herself on the table.

I was on my feet and by her side in record time. Taking her hand, making sure she had not burned herself, I helped her to the table and sat across from her.

Her eyes had begun to sink into their sockets, and her cheek bones became more prominent by the day. Pale skin stretched thin against every bone that stuck out of her body. Her eyes had become clouded and her hair coarse and thin. It was a wonder to me that she was still alive.

I watched her for a moment before suddenly remembering, "Why are you home? I thought they had you working in the fields today."

"T-T...They," She cleared her throat. "They sent me home."

"Why?" I pushed further.

She shied away from my eyes, "There was an... accident."

I began to lose my patience by this point, "What kind of accident?" I spoke through gritted teeth.

"I-I fainted…"

I was beyond disbelief, "Piper, what has been going on? Why are you not healing from opening the portal?"

"When… When I opened the portal, it drained nearly all of my magic, and with people being so hard on magic users, magic is disappearing, so the ability to-" She rambled.

"Just spit it out Piper!" I snapped.

She nodded hesitantly, gathering her thoughts into one place.

Carefully she placed her frail hand on mine and met my eyes, "Journey… I'm dying."

~6~

Tristan's POV:

THE STREETS WERE empty, which was unusual for the time of day. It was almost an eerie atmosphere as a breeze blew through the treeless streets. No soul was to be found around the medieval buildings towering higher than I had ever seen buildings go. It fascinated me to say the least.

"Tristan." Ozara called, pulling me away from my thoughts.

I met her teal eyes before looking away, heat rising in my cheeks.

"As I was saying, I'm worried Journey doesn't understand the fight she is creating with the Queen…" I zoned out again.

Everyone worries about Journey, and Journey does not want to be worried about. I understand she needs time to heal, but I also understand she does not realize that. I wish people would just leave her be and let her go through her life as she wishes.

Ozara grabbed my upper arm. My eyes jumped from her to the group of guards in front of me.

"Milku told you." I could feel my heart sinking in my chest.

I had always hoped one day I could be there for Ozara in her time of need as she is there for me in mine. Yet as time went on, my hope of that day coming dimmed.

She nodded and tried to keep me moving, her expression cold and stern. She was stating her authority to them in efforts to keep them quiet.

"Well, well… if it isn't Beast Boy and his little guard." The head guard called, stepping in front of us.

Fire began to burn in Ozara's eyes as her undeniable temper flared. They were getting under her skin, and that was their plan.

Ozara shoved past him, hitting her shoulder against his arm. I followed quickly behind.

"I'd be careful, Sweets. That man is a monster!" He yelled after us.

His name for Ozara made my own anger rise more than his comment of me. It was disrespectful the way he treated people, and he used his position to get away with it.

"Why you little-" Before Ozara could say much more, I took her by the hand and began to lead her away.

After leaving their earshot, I whispered, "Leave it alone. It's not worth it."

Ozara spun around to face me, making me stop in my tracks. She was attractive, but she was more so strong and independent. Her temper was once feared all over the land, and though she kept everything behind a lock in her heart, every so often she allowed it to see a moment of freedom. Her teal eyes held strength, but also loneliness after returning to civilian life.

Her ash blonde hair had grown just past her shoulders. She was my height or a little shorter but would win any fight between us. Not only was she highly trained in combat but mastered the art of interrogation in her years of being a commander.

"Tristan, are you listening?" I met her eyes.

I swallowed a lump in my throat and nodded.

"Don't lie to me." She was serious.

"Don't worry about it if it isn't worth it."

A harsh expression came over her face, "How can you say that? They have been treating you like this since we arrived back from Althea's Realm."

I shook my head, a power tempting me to lash out, but I held it in with as much concentration as I could muster, "It is nothing I have not heard before. It doesn't bother me."

Liar...

I tried to give her a reassuring smile, but I knew she could see right through it.

I stole my gaze back and began to walk away. She came running after me and grabbed my hand.

"Tristan, tell me what is wrong. You have been getting more distant the longer we are here and I'm starting to get worried about you."

I met her pleading eyes and watched as the confidence faded from her stance leaving a vulnerable woman in her place.

"I-I just don't understand how I deserve this."

Her head tilted slightly, making her hair fall over part of her face, "What do you mean?"

"You and Milku have both been so quick to defend me against these people when what they say is true. Are you not afraid that I will lose control and hurt you?"

With a straight face she answered, "No."

"Why not!" I screamed, before backing away, running my fingers through my thick hair, "Why not…" I whispered, looking away from her, "I am a… monster, after all…"

She took a few steps towards me and placed her hand to the side of my head, maneuvering my face to look at her.

"Listen to me, Tristan. I've met far worse monsters than you. If you were to ever be compared to those people, you would be an angel among them." She paused, "No one can be a perfect hero, and even if they can, it does not make them a good person. What your father did to those people does not mean you are like him."

She placed her hand on my chest, and I could feel my heartbeat quicken, "What defines you is who you choose to be. And at the moment, you are choosing to be a good man. That proves you are not a monster, because your heart is good, and you have no drive for evil."

I stayed quiet, thinking of what she said, but a voice in the back of my head still whispered.

Monster…

"Ladies and Gentlemen, if I could please have your attention." The voice echoed through the streets from the courtyard.

Ozara took her hand from my chest and walked curiously around me. I followed her to the crowd of people gathered around the fountain.

"I am Queen Amoret. I come on behalf of the Kingdom of Tuhe and the Army of Resmen."

I had almost forgotten about our ally in the war. It had been a long time since we last saw her, but I could already tell a lot had changed.

Amoret dressed in battle armor, similar to what Ozara used to wear. Her deep red hair had grown long but was pulled back. Gray eyes swiped over the crowd, looking out among the people. With the pride in her stance, I knew Amoret had finally taken over her kingdom. And it was easy to tell she did it alone.

"Tuhe and the King of Resmen are joining together to defeat a monster in their region."

It can't be...

"We are looking for volunteers willing to travel to a small village in Resmen called Everwinter. Among the Frostforth mountains of this village, a creature, the locals call the Beast of Everwinter needs to be captured and executed."

He's a monster...

There's evil in his blood...

Nothing but a beast...

"We are looking for fighters to-"

Before she could finish her sentence, my hand shot up, "I'll go! I'll fight the Beast of Everwinter."

I wanted to fight. I was terrified and shaking under my cloak, but I had to do it. I was ready, maybe not prepared to watch my father die, but ready.

However, I was not prepared to see the woman next to me raise her hand. When I looked at her, heat rose into my cheeks and I knew the look she had in her teal eyes. She was both ready and prepared.

~ ~ ~

I barely noticed how dirty the stable was as my thoughts were stuck in a frenzy. I glanced over the map Milku had flattened out over a bale of hay.

"You'll cross the river here." She touched her long finger a few inches west from the center, "Nero should be able to take you the rest of the way after a small break."

I glanced down the long aisle, listening to the horses nicker to one another, watching their breath turn to smoke in the chilled air of the night, "What if we don't make it in time?"

"Please!" A tall, bulky man with a heavy accent walked forward with a horse's reins secured tightly in his hand, "Nero is the most reliable and the fastest horse in New Hollow." He scratched his red beard as he handed the reins to Milku.

The steed was tall, his back reaching well past my head. His white coat had been cleaned of dust and his mane, which hung over the browband of his bridle, was not bleached yellow from the sun. He was a pristine picture that held pride in his stance.

"If any horse can get you to the Sacred Forest, it's Nero." Milku turned to the creature, "Isn't that right, Handsome?" She scratched under his forelock.

Nero blinked at me with his intelligent brown eyes, before shaking his head, making his mane fly everywhere. I jumped back, worried he was going to hurt me.

"I have to say, out of everything, I definitely did not expect you to be afraid of horses.

Asmund came through the stable entrance with Piper leaning heavily on him.

"Ready to go?" Asmund's calm voice filled the air of the stable's vaulted ceiling, making the horses stand quietly.

Without saying a word, I nodded.

After hooking up a wooden cart to Nero's harness, I helped Piper into the back while Asmund climbed onto the driver's seat.

Milku placed her hand on Nero's nose, and offered him a sugar cube with the other.

"Take care of them, Nero," She whispered, "There is a reason the forest has stayed sacred all of this time."

~7~

Asmund's POV:

I STEERED NERO through the shallow ford in the river. By this point in the trek to the Sacred Forest, the trees around us began to get dense and overgrown brush leaked into the barely marked path.

I paused and let Nero take a drink as he began to get a steady hold on the slippery rocks on the bank. He was a sure-footed steed and steady despite the flimsy cart being pulled behind him.

Glancing back after moving to secure land, I smiled at Journey sleeping peacefully next to Piper, who was also sleeping.

Remembering my conversation with Journey, I smiled, thinking back to when we had rested a few hours before we reached the river.

"What are you thinking of?" I questioned, stealing a glance at her as she sat beside me on the wagon.

She was facing away from me, her loose hair covering her face, "It's just… everything is so different now. I feel almost like I don't belong here anymore. I became so attached to Secret Hollow, I forgot to think of what it would be like to lose it." She sighed, "It carries a familiar feeling of Secret Hollow, but it isn't home."

I chuckled to myself, "That's because even though the place has changed, the people haven't. Sure, there are some newcomers, but the people that made Secret Hollow home, are still welcoming you with open arms. You are thinking too much of what Secret Hollow looks like, you have forgotten a kingdom is made up of its people. Besides, you have changed too. You have grown stronger and wiser in your magic. You have become accepting of it and of those who are different around you."

She spun her head and glanced at me with her stunning green eyes, and I had to look away as heat began to creep up my face.

"What would I do without you?" She questioned, a teasing smirk coming across her pink face.

I teased her back, "Probably get some rest…"

Her face became sober, "I cannot sleep… Without the Mystics' Tree shielding me, my magic haunts my mind."

"You will not heal if you do not rest."

She nodded, "I know, but that knowledge does not make the task any easier."

I smiled small, "Just sleep, I am here should you need me."

A smile forced its way onto my face at the memory. I watched her doze lightly, her face cupped in her hand. She looked so peaceful, which was a good sign. It made me think maybe she was slowly moving past everything.

To think the first time I met you, I wanted nothing to do with you. My plan was to never become involved in your life, only to use you to end my guilt. But you were as good for me then as you are now. I have been swept into this crazy adventure of yours, and slowly the guilt is being pushed away by the light you give me. I care for you more than I ever thought I would be able to.

Before I could continue my thought process, Nero yanked at the reins. As the leather strips slid through my hands, I grabbed them quickly, careful not to frighten the stallion.

Nero's black nostrils flared, and his milky eyes were outlined with white.

Whatever he smelled was close, and he would not travel with ease.

I tried to urge him forward, knowing we were very close to the Sacred Forest.

Dismounting the wagon, I went up and gripped the base of his bridle. Hesitantly, the stallion followed forward. He was a bright creature, but still obedient, but that didn't stop his soaking skin from trembling beneath my touch.

My anxiousness leaked into my mind as the wind began to nip at my bare arms that were exposed from beneath my cloak. Night was falling fast and though we were far from any settlement, bandits still lurked around these parts.

Over time, my nerves settled in the pit of my stomach, which helped encourage Nero along. We crossed the opening between the tress and entered the forest. Once under the cover of the trees, I mounted back into the wagon.

I had barely gotten Nero back into a gentle walk when a howl sounded through the trees. I knew it was not the wind, but it sounded as though it was only echoing through the trees. It was loud enough, however; to cause Journey to stir from her sleep. Nero began to pace in the confines of the cart's shafts. He gave a slight rear, baring his teeth at the bit and yanked the reins from my hands.

He took off, throwing Journey off balance and to the floor of the cart. I wrestled for the reins as Nero sprinted forward. It was clearly not his fastest gait but was still dangerous when taking the tight turns between the tall trees.

Journey grasped the side rail of the wagon and held her hand out, letting it sprinkle with the gold liquid of her magic.

"Stop!" She yelled, echoing through the forest.

Nero flipped his ears back at the sound of her voice, a gentle expression coming over his face, and slowed long enough for me to gather the reins. As I pulled him to a halt, he lowered his head, blew out a puff of air into the dirt, and sighed.

After he finished, I nodded a thanks to Journey, "I did not mean to wake you."

"It wasn't your fault. Besides, I don't need to sleep for long. As long as my magic can replenish, then I will be fine." She paused and looked to her surroundings, "Do you know where we are?"

I shook my head, "Nero took us off the path."

Another breeze rustled the branches above us. Journey stood, allowing her hands to light up the darkness. Nero's ears perked up, his nostrils flaring as he blew white smoke into the air.

Laying my hand cautiously on the hilt of my sword, I steadied Nero.

At least a dozen of them fell from the treetops. They surrounded us, cloaked by the darkness. From the sparse light of Journey's magic, I could see flashes of the tan creatures.

I felt multiple hands grab me and shove me to the broken soil.

A ringing in my ears shot a sharp pain through my head, but my focus was stuck on Journey struggling nearby. Her yelling ceased eventually.

I lifted my head as they lit the torches around us.

The man who was clearly in charge was tanner than the rest. He had long blond hair that was shaved on one side, exposing his elf ears which curled long past the back of his head. His misty green eyes were that of the fog covering Secret Hollow in the early light of the morning. A serious expression came over his face as he began giving orders.

"Check the wagon, and steady that horse." His command was short but taken with pure authority by his group.

One of the thin girls, whose face was covered with heavy paint to camouflage her, walked gracefully on her bare feet. Her thick, braided blonde hair looked like the matted mane of a lion tucked behind her short, pointed ears.

While the woman was searching through the bags left in the cart from its previous voyage, the leader muttered to one of the men holding me down, "They have brought the one the humans call Althea. She should be a fortune at the market."

I jerked at the thought, knowing the man's attention was not on me. Though he stumbled, he quickly retained his grip tighter than before.

"Sir, there is another maiden…" The woman called.

The man marched heavily on his bare feet to the wagon, peering over the side paneling with ease.

Piper's voice was barely audible, indicating her rapid decline in health, "P-*ple*- please… l-l…et the-*go*…." Her voice was ghostly.

"Grace given from the Elders…" The man whispered

He spun to the others, "Unhand these people."

One of the elves questioned him, "But Macken-"

"Unhand these people and get on your knees…" He glanced back at Piper with a pure wonderment lightening his eyes that was otherwise non-existent, "Our queen has come home."

~8~

Ozara's POV:

NIGHT HAD FALLEN over the mountains of Frostforth. A quiet, almost eerie wind blew through the streets of the small village.

The little wooden houses with their roofs covered in snow, sat quaint under a clearing from the tall pines. A wooden fence, broken in more ways than one, surrounded the homes nearest to the forest where we made camp. It did not offer the people much protection from the dark forest, which almost seemed to linger behind me as I walked.

My feet crunched in the cold, and my arms ached from the heavy firewood. It had been too long since I was out in the battlefield.

I approached the camps and saw many groups huddled around a small fire. We had made a safe, yet treacherous voyage to the Region of Resmen. We were lucky to reach land in time to make camp as night was falling quickly.

I had never been to Resmen, but I had heard stories from the travelling merchants that once filled the streets of Evnock.

Evnock... The name haunted my mind the same as Calvin's devilish grin.

If it were not for Journey and her friends, I believed I would not be fighting in this fight. In a way they seemed to rescue me from the dark kingdom, though it was not my choice to leave. Even though I knew Calvin was sealed away in Althea's Realm, I could feel him lingering behind me at night, similar to that of the dark forest haunting me.

A shiver ran down my spine, partly from the chill of the wind and partly from the thought of Calvin. He was an evil man, and nothing would change that.

I shook the thoughts of him from my mind, remembering he should not have the ability to take them up as much as he did.

Rounding the corner, following a long row of tents, I smiled.

Tristan sat near a small fire; his black hair dusted with fresh snow. His reddish curls had grown out and were now being illuminated by the flames. His tan skin lightened in the cold months in Secret Hollow

Fire dancing in his lime eyes, he spotted me and flashed a charismatic smile my way. I wondered if being here brought up memories of a bad time the way they did for me when I thought of Evnock.

My eyes shied away from his gaze, suddenly becoming aware of his eyes watching me.

As I approached, Tristan stood and crossed the small opening. He removed some of the firewood from my arms and nodded a thanks. One of the limbs caught his coat, revealing the slightest bit of his scarred arms he tried so hard to hide.

After we both threw our share of dry wood into the fire, watching the flames expand in the night air, I sat on a fallen log, shivering slightly from the wind cutting through my few layers of clothing.

Before Tristan sat down, he removed a blanket from his tent and placed it around my shoulders.

"Thank you." I met his eyes.

He flashed a dazzling smile.

Stop hiding from me...

Across the fire was another soldier that camped in our small section of the outskirts.

The man looked young, but was probably older than he appeared, like many elves. His skin was darker than most, meaning he was probably from the Southern forests. Straight blonde hair hung far past his thin shoulders. He was taller and skinnier than many of the Southern elves preferred, but each had its differences similar to the Metronite tribes.

His deep brown eyes met mine, "So, Lady Ozara, will you be joining us on Tristan's excursion?"

"What excursion?"

He furrowed his brow, "Tristan's plan to leave camp." He said as if I was supposed to know what he was speaking of.

"Alarik..." Tristan's voice was somewhere between a scowl and a whisper.

Letting the blanket fall from my shoulders, I turned to Tristan, eyes widened, "What is this plan he speaks of?"

Alarik's eyes went wide as he looked between Tristan and me, "Oh… She wasn't supposed to know… I'm going to head in for the night." He jumped from his seat and sealed himself away in his tent.

"By Heavens, Alarik…" Tristan ran his hand through his thick hair, revealing the creases forming in his skin.

"You were not planning on telling me." I spoke softly, trying to see beneath his cryptic expression.

Tristan sighed, "I was… but I did not think you would agree."

"It would help to know what I would be agreeing to."

He gave a slight nod, "I think we need to leave. Go through the village before the others."

"Why would we do such a thing! It is committing treason-"

"Because the townspeople will recognize me!" His voice rose, "…when they look at me, they only see the beast's blood which runs through my veins." Staring at his scarred arms being illuminated by the light of the fire, he zoned out.

"Tristan… what are you not telling me?"

He refused to meet my eyes, "These people do not know what I am. But if we go with them, they will…"

"You have not been able to control it…" I whispered.

He shook his head, "Nor the magic I possess. Since we have returned from Althea's Realm, the beast within me has become too much to bear… if these people find out what I am, they will send me home. If I am not here… even I do not know how terrible my father will treat them," He took an unsteady breath, "These people do not have to die… no more have to die trying to accomplish what I am destined to do."

My voice got softer as magic began to glow from his lime eyes, "And what is that?"

He looked up at me, his eyes hollow and empty. The look sent a shiver down my spine, and as I looked longer, I knew this man before me was not Tristan.

"I am to be the one to kill my father."

~9~

THE ELVEN PEOPLE separated us from each other with talk of a gala being held at the palace. Two very beautiful elves escorted me through the forest.

The forest settlement was much different than I imagined. From the look of the guards which attacked us in the forest, I expected a much more rural tribe. This was not the case, though. Homes were built out from the trees with moss growing down their stone bricks. Carefully carved wooden doors and crafted stained glass christened every house. The people walked with their heads held high along the cobbled streets that set partially buried under a layer of moss. Lamps lined the streets, pushing away the darkness created by the density of the forest, leaving the area with a green hue.

The people were dressed in intricate gowns of bead work and embroidery stitching. Many had the signature blonde hair and forest eyes common to this tribe; however, it also made the others who travelled from other tribes stand out in lower rankings. Each elf walked with their own simple stride, and many of the elders used the aid of a polished walking stick carved carefully with intricate designs. There was a sort of elegance of the place which reflected the silence of the air. Besides the crickets chirping and an odd bird singing high in the pines, there was not a sound.

After following the elves through the elaborate structures and thick foliage, we arrived at what I would only imagine to be the palace.

It was a cross shaped building large enough to house the entire forest within its walls comfortably. Beautiful glass work covered the building's windows and mossy stone made up the structural walls. The path leading to the front entrance was lined with trimmed bushes and small trees, strung with lanterns. Towering in the middle of the building, was a glass dome with lights hanging above it from the trees. The enchanting sight stole my breath.

The elves motioned me off the path, walking through the flowered ground to the back of the palace. As we rounded the corner to the shadow of the palace, chills encased my body, making the hair on the back of my neck stand up.

I spun, but only saw the lights staring back at me. There was a feeling that lingered after in this place and I could not quite think of what it was, or why it seemed familiar.

Two guards opened the large doors. I followed them inside, underneath a soaring hall painted green with murals above each panel of gold chair railing. A small room sat quietly to the side. The guards stood by its door as one of the elves closed it behind us.

"Have a seat." One said with a sweet smile.

Hesitantly, I sat in one of the available chairs. The room was a seating room acting as a dressing room, possibly changed with the gala being under way.

"So, where are my friends?" I questioned as the two rummaged through the shelves of the armoire.

One of the elves, a brunette with almond colored eyes, turned towards me and smiled, "They are here also. Our queen is preparing for her crowning and the handsome guard with you is with some of the male staff also preparing for the gala. Which is what you should be doing instead of asking so many questions."

The other elf, who was thin and lanky, walking with no grace in her step, came over and began trying to untangle my knotted hair, "You must look your best for tonight."

I winced as the elf, I believe was called Alva, pulled a knot through the makeshift brush.

"Why such a big party?" I asked through clenched teeth.

The brunette, who Alva called Avery, turned and started to wipe my face with a damp cloth, "In the elven culture, we elves are not born with magic like you humans. If an elf is born with magic, the forest will take it before they reach marrying age. When our magic is sacrificed to the forest, we retain our safety of living within it."

Alva spoke up, "Our ancestors' legend tells us we are to crown a new leader every new century. The leader will be an elf of marrying age who was born with a full amount of magic. It is said when the forest senses the elf's magic, it will not take it. This elf is to be our next leader."

"Many magic users do not show their power until marrying age, but elves age slower than humans. Years ago, each of the female elves, as it alternates every century, were taken to the palace to be examined." Alva finished with my hair and began braiding and pinning it to my head.

Avery batted her large, dewy eyes in the mirror, "It was discovered both Piper and her sister, Alara, held extreme magic abilities. However, Alara is younger than Piper, and she was not of marrying age. The elders declared Piper as our rightful heir."

"Upon hearing this news, Piper fled in the night and has not been seen since," Alva paused, stepping back and admiring my hair, "We all believed Alara would take the throne… that is until you brought our queen home, where she will rule until the next elf arises."

My thoughts played with my head, *until she becomes lost...*

~10~

Tristan's POV:

WE ARRIVED IN Everwinter right as the sunlight peaked over the snow-covered mountains.

The place was just as I remembered…

Houses were plastered into the sides of the mountains, spiraling around its rigid cliffs and snowy peaks. Each house was supported with dark wood, though the houses were not stable, and gave minimum protection against the wind. The streets were once cobbled, but now even covered in snow year around, holes and loose stones caused a hazard to all that walked across them. The people here were left to their own lives, making money in any way they were able. This village was an accurate representation of how many of the villages struggled.

Resmen did not take heed in how its fellow regions compiled and ran. Unlike Kocala, Resmen had one leader. While the Regions King sat high on his throne of gold and gems, protected from the cold in fleece lined coats, the villages scattered in the large region were stuck in a sense of poverty. No one travelled to other villages for help, for you would either run out of supplies and not finish the trip, or the village you sought to enter would not take you in. Boat fares out of the region were high, as good, sturdy boats were hard to come by. All of the lakes and in the ocean nearest the coast was ice, making the fish the only good source of food and income. Few crops grew, as it was dark most of the time, with sunlight only coming in the morning and was usually covered with a thick layer of fog. It was a region stuck in an age of stone and poverty, for they also outlawed many of the magic users. It was this town that finally realized their need for magic, but still turned their backs on it.

    I looked down at my snow-covered boots. Alarik was filing behind me and Ozara stood beside me so as to not lose her balance on the icy streets

    My hood covered most of my face, and I hoped it would be enough to get us through the drawn-out village.

"Tristan it has been over twelve years since these people have seen you. Would you take off that annoying hood?" Ozara's tone was harsh from our conversation last night.

I swallowed a lump in my throat and did as she asked, realizing there were not many people around. I already knew my eyes were glowing as the beast within me begged to be freed.

We continued through the village slower than necessary despite heading straight through without any detours. Eventually, though, as I feared, an older man recognized me.

"Aye, you three!" His raspy voice hollered.

Ozara was the first to turn to the man, letting out a scowl as she did.

"I don't know what your friend told ya, but he isn't welcome in these parts." He was leaning heavily on his walking stick and spitting as I tried to make out what he was saying through his thick accent.

"We are merely passing through on our way to the mountains." Ozara remained calm.

Alarik stood back, still not aware of the full reason we left the camp.

Ozara stepped in front of me, challenge lingering in her voice. Out of everything I admired about her, I was still unsure about her sense of never quitting, "Sir, if you would only let us continue, we will be on our way."

By this time a crowd began to gather, some who remembered me, and others who had only heard stories. Many of them readied their swords while others froze with terrified expressions.

I could feel my magic aching to be released and the beast within me was getting anxious as the man took a step towards Ozara.

Before anyone else had the chance to speak, a man shoved through the crowd towards Ozara, his sword drawn.

With the magic burning inside of me and the instant reaction to protect Ozara, I released my magic. Without a second thought, we had all disappeared.

~ ~ ~

Ozara's POV:

It had finally stopped snowing long enough to build a small fire. I was worried it would not last long as we were camped on the outskirts of Everwinter, higher up on the mountain.

I watched Tristan, who poked at the fire with a small stick, moving the kindling around to keep the fire going. His eyes glowed with a trail of green mist against his pink cheeks. He was ashamed, frustrated, maybe even mad at himself. It was hard to read him when he got like this.

Once the man came towards me in the village, Tristan used his magic to teleport us to the outskirts of Everwinter. He saved my life, along with unnecessary fighting with the locals, but he did not see it as so. Whether he lost control or did it on purpose, he had not spoken a word since it happened.

Darkness had covered the sky, with no stars in sight and the only light in the area was that which flickered across Tristan's furrowed brow.

"Do you want to tell me what happened?" I asked quietly, careful to not wake Alarik who was sleeping in the tent nearby.

He hung his head and dropped the stick to the ground, "Not particularly."

I stayed silent as he lifted his glowing eyes to look at me, "I have put us in immense danger."

"You saved our lives today."

"I could have killed us!" He yelled, then winced peering over his shoulder to Alarik's tent.

He was fighting a battle I could not be sure he would win.

"It was dangerous to reveal my magic and it was dangerous to bring you both along with me."

"We chose to come… you did not force us." I took a breath, "Besides… I do believe you were right when you said only you could defeat your father."

"But in a way, I believe even I am not powerful enough to defeat him."

I sighed and gripped the hem of my sleeve, "Than I can use my magic… together I am sure we could figure out something." My voice was barely audible.

Silence lingered in the air mixing between us and the fire.

"W-What do you mean… 'your magic'?" He hesitated.

I sighed, watching my white breath swirl into the night air, "I cannot remember if I have mentioned this to you before, but when I was very small my parents died in a bandit raid. The raid was done by Metronites. These Metronites were not like the ones we know now, they were wild…savage. This tribe was made of outcasts and runaways, which in some cases I suppose would be good, but in this particular moment, it was not. They raided our cart because they had Nova's relic, and they believed it chose me. The leader thought if the relic chose me as its host, then he could sell me for a fortune."

Tossing another log into the fire, I took a long breath before continuing, "They ended up selling me when I reached marrying age. Before the buyer could appear, I ran away and joined the guard academy, took my birth name, and slipped into the shadows."

"Took your birth name?" He questioned, making me lose my train of thought.

"Y-Yes. My given name is Ozara but when the… tribe… took me in they changed it, afraid someone would come looking for me. It would probably be a name you are familiar with as it is from these parts. They-They called me Parnaa."

His brow furrowed, and he clenched his fists, "A prize."

I nodded, "It was all I was to them… anyway, eventually after being stationed in Evnock, Calvin learned of my secret. The… spell… he used on Journey, he practiced for a very long time on me. For a long time, I believed there was no magic left within my body, but I am still alive so there must be some."

"I wish you would have told me sooner. Magic could have made your life so much easier."

"I never learned to use my magic… I could not bring myself to after that. I was just like the wolves in that tribe. A runaway, an outcast. I was a coward. I did not want the responsibility. Not then, not now. I can take the responsibility for a patrol of guards… but the whole world?" My voice dropped.

When Tristan was upset, he distanced himself or became silent. No one could reach through his thoughts. I was different. When I was upset, I became weak because I wept. I wept enough to make me vulnerable.

I expected Tristan to distance himself as everyone else did. I was a broken person hiding behind a mask, not the person he thought I was.

Instead of responding as I expected, he rose and came beside me before wrapping me in a warm embrace.

"Yet," He whispered, his breath warm against my skin, "I believe if anyone could do it, it would be you."

~11~

Asmund's POV:

PEOPLE STARTED TO crowd into the ballroom of the ancient castle. They were all dressed in gowns or embellished suits. Some wore masks and concealed their identities while others, like me, had refused them.

I stuck close to the outer wall and watched as the palace workers and elders went in and out.

The palace aids which assisted me were not eager to stay. I had snuck away and wandered the halls, looking for a gem I had only read about, but which might have the power to fix all our problems. Sadly, I could not locate it, and I feared they moved it somewhere safe because of the party.

The Sacred Forest was built on the myth of the forest consuming the Elves magic, when, in truth, it was the elders using a gem that stored magic energy. The gem could only take premature magic, meaning those who are born with exceptional strong magic, were spared and crowned for it.

"Good evening." One of the workers nodded, handing me a heavy glass of spring water.

I nodded my thanks, "A lovely one, indeed."

These people were blind to the corruption of their elders. If I could get my hands on the gem, we could open the portal and save Damon's life.

I scanned the ballroom, which at the moment was only elders and higher officials that stayed in the castle. As my eyes reached the far wall of the room, my thoughts subsided as my eyes landed on her.

The front pieces of her hair were braided back in efforts to tame her wild honey curls. Tangled curls melted down her shoulders to her waist. She held her head high, not with pride but to make comfort easier with the green silk tied around her neck. A forest green dress danced to the floor, as it was much too long for her short frame. The lace sleeves were also too long and hung past her hands in pointed tips. The back was open down to the end of her hair but covered with a few fine gold chains reaching from one shoulder to the other attached to metal pieces made to resemble feathers falling down her shoulders.

I watched her from the corner of my eye, sipping my water every so often. Eventually, I caught her eye as she closed her conversation with the elder. She began to walk over to me, moonlight glistening against her broad features, and her dress swaying around her quickened stride. Her dazzling emerald eyes sparkled with a passion I had not seen in some time. A blush creeped onto her tan cheeks when she realized she had held my gaze longer than usual, she smiled. Her smile was beautiful, one she saved for special moments with special people.

And in that moment when she smiled, showing she was fighting through the darkness and winning, it made one thing clear to me.

She was beautiful, but she was strong, willing to fight any brokenness she felt, and it was that moment when I realized how far I had fallen for her.

~ ~ ~

Journey's POV:

The ballroom bustled with people by this time of the night, nearly midnight. Piper was being serious when she said this forest came alive at night.

The palace was a beautiful structure, but the ballroom was the part that stole my breath. A glass dome towered above us, moonlight shining upon the light birch floors, and detailed paintings. Archways were embedded around the room and candles had been lit on the walls to provide some light, but most was provided from up above. The stars twinkled above, though separated by the glass.

As more people entered the room, I noticed their attire. The women wore dresses that flowed on their bodies instead of hugging them too tightly. And the men wore embellished suits and vests with tall boots.

My eyes wandered to Asmund as he watched the crowd among us, and my face held a heat it had not before.

His black hair was trimmed and combed back away from his tan face, with few pieces left to frame it. His warm skin glowed in the candlelight as the silver specks danced around his dark eyes. He was dressed in a white button down and a black vest embroidered in gold vines stitched across the dark surface. Tall boots accentuated his height and gave him a cleaner appearance I was not used to.

"So, what do you think of this place?" Asmund returned his attention to me.

I smiled, lost in thought, "What should I know of it? I have been here equally as long as you."

"There is magic here. Being a magic user, you should be able to sense the type of aura given off it. Similar to how you feel the presence of the Mystics' Tree."

I closed my eyes and concentrated. I did feel the slightest bit of magic in the air, but it was not the pleasant feeling I felt beneath the Mystics' Tree.

Keeping my eyes closed, I spoke, "It is quiet, but not peaceful." I sighed, losing the connection.

"How could something be quiet, but not peaceful?" He questioned, tilting his head with a small smirk.

I thought for a moment, "Like when someone is being quiet, but you know they are watching you with every intent to change you. Or when someone says something, and it feels wrong to question or respond to them. Enjoying someone's company but being too worried your words will cause them to leave."

"You seem to be talking about someone in particular. Is this true?"

"Yes, Damon. I enjoy his company but wonder how long it will remain. He seems so happy when he speaks, it seems wrong to ruin that when I do not understand something. Or when he watches me and thinks of all the things he can show me to change my mind about this world. Sometimes it just becomes too much."

"You talk of him as if he is here. Is your magic speaking to you?"

I stared at my hands, hidden by the long bell sleeves, "I feel as though he is here, like I could turn around and see him walking towards me, but I do not see or hear him like I do the others."

"The others?"

I nodded, "The other voices. They scream and claw at my mind. They are what keep me up at night and when I use my magic, they are able to find me like that day in the field."

He placed his hand on my shoulder and met my eyes, "How often do you listen to these voices?"

I let out a small laugh, "I don't try to. Though there are some I do not mind. One helped me come to the conclusion of the prophecy Nola told me. If only I could actually fulfill it."

"You mentioned it to me before, but that was long ago."

"In the end there would be one life lost, and it would be mine."

He searched my face with his pleading black eyes, "A life lost? Journey, how far are you really willing to go to bring Damon back?"

I sighed, "Prophecy or no prophecy, I honestly believe in my heart I would do whatever it takes to bring him back. If it takes my life then so be it. He is the one who deserves to live, not me."

Before Asmund could respond, the Elder's voice came over the crowd.

He was older but did not look it. His hunched back made him shorter than the others, but his long ears reached well behind his head, making him stand out among the crowd. He wore a green cloak with intricate designs over simple brown garments. His long blond hair was pulled into a bun at the back of his head, braids coming from his neck and pulled into it. Piercings ran up the base of his ears.

"Ladies and Gentlemen," His disfigured voice spoke loudly, "May I ask for us to commence this event. Before the Queen is revealed to you, she has asked for you all to eat and dance that you may be merry when she arrives."

After the small announcement, music began to fill the halls, and people filled the floors with chatter and dancing.

We waited for some time with no sign of Piper, which had me worried.

"J-Journey…" Asmund stuttered.

Wiping my nerves from the palms of my hands, I turned, my breath catching as his hand was held out to me.

"May I have this dance?" As heat spread across his face, he refused to look at me.

I hesitated, watching him quietly. With as much as I had put him through, he still acted like this. He somehow still disregarded the brokenness I held.

Taking a deep breath, I placed my trembling hand in his. I allowed him to lead me to the center of the room, though I grew nervous.

He placed my hands on his broad shoulders and swept me into a simple sway to the music. The tone was familiar but lost in a different world.

I met his eyes, noticing a sorrow in them, but not thinking much of it.

"Does this make you uncomfortable?" He asked, resulting in a small smile from me.

Realizing he was serious I dropped the smile. "Why do you ask?"

He gave a small chuckle, "You are shaking under my touch."

It was then I noticed the trembling of my hands as they laced around his shoulders.

Shaking my head, I tried to calm myself, "No, it does not make me uncomfortable. I just am not used to letting myself get close to people."

Can I trust you to hold my heart? I know you would not lie to me, but am I willing to fall blindly into you. I know in my heart, you would not leave my side, but do you need me by yours? Will you listen to me and love me, even when I am a broken mess, as I usually am? Are you willing to look past my flaws? Am I willing to let you see that far into my heart?

I looked to my feet as my questioning thoughts continued, *I've been hurt. I don't want the pain this could bring, but I don't want the loneliness of leaving you. Will you abandon me like all the others? Will you stay with me, no matter what I do wrong?*

I felt his hand so delicately leave from my waist to lift up my chin, meeting my eyes with a reassuring gaze.

"Do not listen to the thoughts in your head. Why do you not let yourself get close to people?" He asked quietly.

I could not bring myself to look away from him, "B-Because eventually I would disappoint them, and they will leave me."

"You should know if you were to ever disappoint me, I will not hold it against you. We are both humans, we both make mistakes. You are imperfect just as I am." He paused and smiled sweetly, "As I watched you walk over to me this evening, I saw strength. I was impressed to say the least. You are going through enough darkness, anyone would give up in your position, but you don't. I felt pride as I watched you this evening."

I felt tears well in my eyes, threatening to fall on my cheeks. Quickly, before I could let the tears fall, I buried my face in Asmund's shoulder.

I felt him chuckle again before resting his head against mine.

The music continued for some time before fading out. Our moment ended sooner than we both wanted, but the music went faster as the elves around us began a cultural dance Piper had spoken of.

Asmund, still having my hand in his, tried to replicate their movements, pulling me along in his plan.

As we attempted to mimic their movements, it only left us in a fit of laughter. It felt nice to laugh after not doing so in such a long time.

"Excuse me, Sir." An older gentleman approached us, interrupting our fun.

"I hate to break your enjoyment up, but I am dying to ask Lady Althea for a dance. And this dance of all dances would be a tremendous honor."

Still having my hand secured in his, I felt Asmund give my hand a small squeeze before releasing it, "Very well." His deep voice grumbled.

"Thank you, kind Sir." The man came and proceeded to lead me into the proper dance of the elves, correcting my movements every couple of steps.

The man was definitely older, which considering the aging habits of elves, meant he was ancient. His graying hair seemed coarse as it hung past his shoulders. Green eyes glared at me, they were harsh and cold. His skin was dirty and cracked. His attire and short pointed ears proved him low in the rankings of the forest. There was something familiar about him, that I could not quite recognize.

"Has word spread quickly of my presence here?" I asked, carefully following his circled footsteps, thankful I did not actually have to touch his sickly hands.

"No." He answered plainly.

I squinted my eyes as I watched him, "Then how did you know of it?"

"Word from the queen."

"You have spoken to her!" I almost froze in my path.

He grunted, "Some choice words, yes."

"Why out of everyone here, have *you* been allowed to speak to her?" The words came out harsher than intended.

"A father should be allowed to see his child after all this time…"

This time I did stop in my tracks.

"Though I must ask," He also stopped, leaving the people around us, curious, "Why bring her to the place she once ran from?"

"Because… she is dying." I could hardly say the words.

He looked away nodding his head, "You should not have brought her here. This is Alara's kingdom, and Piper no longer deserves to be Queen."

"As her father, I assumed you would understand the circumstances we were under."

He met my eyes with a stone expression, "I would have let her die and been done with it."

My eyes widened, "How could you say such a thing of your daughter?"

"I lost my daughter the same day I lost my pride. She humiliated me and since then I have not cared about what happens to her."

My magic began to bubble in the pit of my stomach, wishing to be freed as my blood boiled, "If that is how you view your daughter because of her running when too much was put on her shoulders... you seem like a horrible man."

"You really must be careful of what you say, Journey"

The fact he knew my name without me offering it, plus the way it left his cracked lips, made a chill run down my spine.

"Your words are powerful over the emotions of others." He whispered.

"Ladies and Gentlemen!" The music faded away, "May I finally have the pleasure of presenting, our Queen!"

"Such as my words will have power over you."

I tried to ignore him as I watched for Piper. I took a few steps forward, towards the front of the room.

Piper walked to the front of the room, carefully taking the crown from the Elders.

Her father placed a hand on my shoulder, whispering to me with his potent breath, "Long live the Queen."

I spun my head back to Piper, just as the crown slipped from her skeleton hands, and fell to the floor breaking in two.

A gasp spread throughout the crowd, as I shoved between the group of people trying to reach her.

As a clock struck midnight somewhere in the room, Piper stumbled and collapsed to the ground.

~12~

Ozara's POV:

THE WIND WHIPPED my cropped hair around my face. We were high on the mountain tops over Everwinter. It was nearly dawn and the cave sat only a few feet away from us.

"I-I… I think we should wait for the others…" Alarik spoke up.

Tristan shot his head towards him, his eyes trailing with green mist, "I fended him off for years on my own. Who are you to say I cannot do it again?" He challenged.

I spoke up, before Tristan had a chance to continue, "We need a plan. We can't go into this blind."

I had been looking at Alarik the entire time, but when I turned my head towards the cave, I saw the very last of Tristan's back disappear into the darkness.

"Tristan!" My voice called, but he did not listen.

When he did not return, I turned to Alarik.

"You do not have to go in after him, Lady Ozara." His formality with my name reminded me of a darker time.

I sighed and glanced back at the cave.

"Yes, I do. If I don't the beast inside of Tristan will surely be released, and I am not willing to watch Tristan go down the same path as his father. And I fear if I do not, his father will kill him."

"I need you to stay here and keep watch. If the other soldiers come, you cannot let them enter that cave. I don't care if you make it collapse on us, do not let them in."

He stopped me, "How am I supposed to keep them away? I am one elf and I am unarmed."

I removed my sword and scabbard from my hip and tossed it at him, "That will solve part of the problem."

I took my steps slowly towards the entrance and mumbled under the wind, "And if you pray, do so for our return."

Stepping into the darkness, I walked slowly, feeling the footing in front of me before taking another step.

After some time of lurking through the darkness, it became significantly lighter, and shadows began to appear on the wall.

A laugh which was hoarse and broken in parts filled my ears.

"You, my son, are so out of control, you cannot even stand before me and look me in the eyes." Finnegan's voice echoed through the tunnel.

I realized we were deep in the earth as I laid my hand on the rough, stone wall and caught my breath at the sight.

Tristan was knelt before his father. His black hair was dripping with sweat. The green trail from his eyes was as vibrant as the moon on a clear night. It was only now in the dim light I noticed his skin was growing pale and the bags under his eyes had gotten much darker.

"Tristan…" I whispered; thankful my voice did not echo.

His father was worse. I once expected to see a beast, mangled and broken, but he was quite the opposite. He looked like a normal man despite the horns and glowing purple eyes. Dark brown hair with red undertones, maybe a shade darker than Tristan's hung down the beast's back. A purple robe with tattered sleeves revealed his badly scarred skin.

Tristan let out a deep scream and jerked to one side, clutching his head. His hands began to glow green, the same as the trail of magic from his eyes.

"Get out of my head!" He yelled through clenched teeth, holding his head down.

A toothy grin spread across Finnegan's face, "As long as your beast controls you, I will never leave your head." The depth of his voice made a shiver run down my spine.

"My mother… my mother believed she could change you… that was before you killed her…"

"I did not kill your mother!" The words boomed, as he gave a smug grin, "But how I wish I did." He clenched his fists.

Tristan cried out in pain, clutching at his chest as tears streamed down his face.

My body moved on its own. I never thought I would make a battle move without thinking, but in that moment, I was not sane.

Before I could stop myself, I slid down beside Tristan. I placed one hand on his back and the other over his which was gripping the fabric covering his chest.

"Stop, please!" The amount of vulnerability in my voice frightened even me.

"What is this…" Finnegan's interest peaked.

"Ozara… leave." Tristan cried.

Finnegan stared at Tristan, causing him to scream again, "I want silence from you."

Tristan's body jerked, as he ran his fingers through his hair, tears dripping onto my arm.

"Tristan don't listen to him. You can fight it, please you have to fight it."

I met the monster's glowing eyes as his eyes went wide for a moment, before a grin stretched over his face.

"I must say..." He took a step off the pile of rubble and gems he was standing on and floated down before me, "It is not every day I meet someone who can look me in the eyes."

"What are you..."

He took a few steps back, looking me up and down, "You are a relic user... and such a kind heart. You don't want to take any responsibility for another's life, yet here you are.

I could not speak. It was like he was in my head, but I did not feel his magic.

"I have left you speechless! Wonderful! I do try my hardest to take the words right out of people's mouth... though it usually involves a much more... torturous way. I must say, Parnaa, can I call you Parnaa? I'm going to anyway. I never thought someone could care for my son the way you obviously do."

"H-How..." My voice dropped.

He watched me with a curious look, though it did not appear in his eyes. Tristan said he was once a loving man, but looking at him now, it seemed as though he lost his ability to comprehend human emotions.

"Do not worry, Parnaa. I cannot read your mind. You relic users are too shielded from my powers. It is Tristan's mind I can see you in. His thoughts are very clear to me and always have been. There are no secrets he can hide from me. He is merely my puppet."

Tristan went still beside me.

"Tristan... don't listen to him."

"He is only doing what he is told," He yelled, "Listen to the power, Son. Embrace what you truly are."

"Tristan! Fight it, please." I placed my hand on his cheek and forced him to face me.

"Embrace the power, Son. And do your deed..." Smirking, Finnegan lifted his head, "Kill her."

Tristan's eyes slowly opened, staring blankly back at me. They were glazed over, and glowing purple.

I snatched my hand back and jumped away, slowly towards the entrance of the cave.

Before I could make it, the ground began to shake beneath us.

My first thought was the soldiers had arrived but stealing a look at Finnegan proved he was the one behind it.

Eventually it increased to the point it knocked Tristan and me to the ground.

I dodged a rock falling from the ceiling and continued trying to put distance between Tristan and me.

I caught a glimpse of him and realized he was not being controlled by his beast, but instead by the monster that was his father.

Tristan began to summon one of his spells from the air, something he himself had never done. He threw the magic towards me, but I jumped away from the targeted area.

The sense of danger overtook my mind, while the concern for Tristan overwhelmed my heart. I knew how to protect myself, but I wanted to protect him more.

Then which is better... seeing him in pain or me being in pain?

A burning filled my body. Before I could make the decision, the truth surfaced. An overwhelming sense of magic overtook me, one that had laid dormant for years.

I no longer wanted to be a warrior, I wanted to be a protector.

~13~

THE WORLD IS harsh. I watched my village burn before my eyes. I was given the ability to protect people, but my magic is driven by revenge. Everyone believes I was abandoned by my village, but it is the opposite. They were abandoned by me. And now I ask myself: how many more must die?

As I am feeling myself fade from this world, I have had time to think. Though I have lost the ability to write, my mind fills my head with stories.

If it was not for the mistakes of Azguard, I would be alive, I would be thriving in front of these people.

Sometimes I believe these people are blinded by their affection for us.

I have been given plenty of time to think of what will happen to me once I fade away. Will they bury me among the fallen warriors? Or will they burn me like the other criminals for the lives I have taken?

I guess it should not matter, for I will not be here to even receive the answer to my question. If the people ever read the list of names given to those whose lives have been taken by my hand, I am sure they will finally understand how terrible a person I am.

If you, my people or my fallen village, are reading this, please remember that as I think of you all on my death bed, I wish I could tell each one of you how sorry I truly am.

~ ~ ~

Calvin's POV:

I watched my brother intently. He slept restlessly. The wound I had given him was beginning to get worse and was resulting in him losing more blood that I was willing to admit.

The air had begun to get stale and reeked with the stench of blood and body odor.

A gripping pain filled my chest. I had seen too many lose their lives, but I could not prepare myself for seeing my brother lose his. Seeing him as vulnerable as he was, brought back so many memories from when we were small. I doubt he would know how painful they were to me.

"Do you remember the night Father chose you to take the crown?"

He only grunted in response but seemed aware of me.

"You were young, not even of marrying age. Considering I reached sixteen years of age, by the day, it would have been two years before you were able to take a bride. Reaching sixteen years of age was a rite of passage for every young prince, but nobody remembered besides Mother. Father called us all together in the throne room. He looked so powerful that day, I almost feared him with the way he sat tall on his throne with Mother to his left side." I sighed.

"Y-You... You had no real knowledge of what was happening. I didn't really at the time either. You looked up and saw your father, I looked up and saw the kind man who took a woman and her child into his care. Over the years, he grew cold towards me, and I should never have been so foolish to believe he ever thought of handing his kingdom over to me."

Choking back tears, I continued, "I can remember the day so vividly, and still struggle to step foot into that throne room."

"Come, My Boy." I mimicked Father's deep voice, "And he motioned to you to come to him and placed his crown on your head. On that day, our fate was sealed."

"I stormed out of the castle. I can still picture the door never closing behind me, and the lack of noise it made as it slowly sat in place, as if not to disturb the moment between a father and his son."

My voice was only a whisper after that tale, "I was gone for weeks building my magic to impress Father…"

"But nobody noticed…"

~ ~ ~

Dear Journey,

I don't believe you will ever read this, because I cannot find someone to brave the wilderness to deliver it to you, but I will keep trying.

Things in Secret Hollow are not good at the moment. The people are in a panic as the Tree, which has not changed colors since you first arrived many years ago, has changed to a lavender cluster of leaves. We cannot think of a good explanation to tell the people, because we do not know why it happened. We are hoping it will calm after a few days.

There has been talk of you being behind this, and the people are not taking to the thought kindly.

Stay safe,
Celeste

~14~

THE HALL WAS plated with a gold chair railing and pressed with a design on each square. The tops were painted a deep green with flowers painted as though they sat in the middle of a field untouched by humans.

It was all a blur. Candlelight being my only means of vision through the dark passage, I walked in a haze. My thoughts were in a mess, and I could not unscramble them.

Piper collapsed and was quickly whisked away by the Elders and guards. I was informed by the healers that their remedies could do nothing for her. I thought bringing her here would help, but one thing was certain no matter what I did…

She was dying.

Piper knew the time was coming, because she requested to see me. But I was afraid to see her.

Turning the corner of the hall, I was allowed through a door off from it. The room was a large bedroom with a wall of windows and a door leading out to the forest. It was dark as the forest covered the moon and stars.

"Piper…" My voiced cracked, only above a whisper as I approached the bed and fell to my knees.

Sweat dripped off her flaming skin, as she laid lifelessly still. Her eyes were clouded over and zoned out at something else in the room. Her blonde hair was pulled over her shoulder with twigs holding its position. Green paint was slathered in tribal markings across her pale skin and was matched with small mint gems stuck to her face. Green lipstick rubbed onto the blanket. Resting on her chest, a glowing green gem was attached to a twisted branch chain.

I took her hand and gave it a light squeeze.

"Journey… please forgive me for leaving you so soon." Her voice was small and had lost its chipper tone.

Tears began to well in my eyes as I tried to stop them from falling, "I should be the one to apologize. I shouldn't have brought you here. If you are to die, I should have at least had the decency to leave you somewhere you were happy."

"I was once happy here…" She looked towards the door, "Could you open a window?"

I rose from beside the large bed and pushed open a couple of the windows, letting the night air blow my hair around my face.

"Have I ever told you why I left?" She asked, clearly living in a different time.

I shook my head, taking a seat at the end of the bed.

"When I was told of my role as queen, I was… ecstatic!" She laughed, before being hit with a violent coughing fit and settling back into the bed, "How excited I was…"

She cleared her throat, "There came a traveler, he went by the name… Oliver. Since I had never left the forest, I did not know there were people outside of it. He had hair as bright as the sun and eyes as pale as moonlight." She zoned out with a lovesick smile, one only granted to those who were remembering their best days.

"He would sit with me at breakfast, as he was welcomed into the palace, and tell me stories of the lands he had visited and the adventures he had had."

She coughed violently, making her voice even more hoarse, "I wanted what he spoke of more than what the elders promised me. So, I ran… and I began the biggest adventure of my life."

Choking back tears, I asked, "Then why did you stay in Secret Hollow?"

"Because I found people who made every day an adventure. I was homesick at first, but the people there made Secret Hollow feel like home. Everything just seemed to fall into place."

She reached to me, and placed her frail hand on mine, "I can feel the magic in you. It is more powerful than anything I have ever felt before. I believe you were meant to change this world, Journey…" She paused, tears slipping down her cheeks, "I just wish I could stay around to see it."

We stayed in silence for some time when I noticed Piper's breathing became labored. I knew by now it was inevitable she would not be returning to Secret Hollow with us.

"Journey… I have one wish only you can fulfill." Her voice was so quiet I strained to hear her.

"Anything."

Her body began to shake violently, chills incasing it, "P-Ple… ease st-op hid-ding your ma…magic." She looked past me to the empty room before her.

"Ol-Oliver?"

I looked out to the empty space and watched as a young-looking man appeared, a bright tinge forming around him.

"Are you ready for an adventure, Piper?" He offered a smile and held out his hand.

At the same time her hand went limp in mine, she appeared next to Oliver. She started out as only a flicker but eventually formed into a bright light.

"Where is Mama?" She asked, taking Oliver's hand in hers.

He rubbed circles on her hand, "She is guarding the forest. Just like she always has."

Piper nodded, and offered one last smile towards me, as one last reassurance to know this wouldn't be the last time, we saw each other, and she disappeared with Oliver.

Tears began to trickle down my face, as I buried it in the soft bedsheets.

"Journey!" Asmund burst into the room and froze.

I met his eyes and through watery vision I watched concern swirl in his eyes as he crossed the room to me.

The wind blew through my hair, making me push it from sticking to my face, "Her last breath was that of the still silence of nature."

Asmund knelt before me, cupping my tear-stained face in his hands.

I fell into his arms and wept. I wept more than I believe I ever had. I wept for Piper and for Damon. I wept every tear I had built up over the years.

"I'm sorry… Journey." He lightly kissed the top of my head, "But we have to leave."

"W-What happened?" I asked trying to take in a deep breath.

He cleared his throat, though I noticed tears in his own eyes, "H-Her father is trying to convince them that we poisoned her…" His voice trailed off, and he hugged me tighter before whispering to me, "They believe you killed her."

~15~

Tristan's POV:

I COULD STILL see everything that was happening, though I could not control what actions my body took. I was my father's puppet.

A bright light came over Ozara and slowly receded back, revealing a stunning picture.

Ozara landed onto the ground, cropped hair pushed away from her teal eyes which glowed with an intensity of magic. Magic dusted her hands and her muscular arms, glowing as she rose.

Her pants were ripped in places from the rocks and dirt was smudged on her face. A pair of large white wings graced her back, each feather having its tip dripped with gold.

Within an instant, Ozara let her magic release. Multiples of her filled the room, confusing my father enough to disable him.

As I was looking at each clone, I could easily tell which was the real Ozara, but I wish I couldn't. As my father controlled my being, he could read my thoughts, meaning he also knew which of the clones was the original.

My body moved without my control. I ran and knocked her to the ground but was too slow as her wings lifted her from the rubble. I was able to grab a handful of her feathers, which were ripped from her wings as she took off, resulting in a yelp from her.

She lifted her hands and created a prison cell around me, but I had already run through it to know it was not real.

Illusion magic! Wait-No!

My father let out a laugh, and sent me charging towards Ozara, knowing she had no way to protect herself. I caught her and shoved her against the wall, conjuring a more powerful version of my magic as I did.

No!

She squirmed in my grasp as my magic charged, knowing my magic energy was low.

You're nothing but a coward…

You're a good man…

A monster…

You would be an angel…

No one could care for my son…

I care about you, I thought that was obvious…

I could hear a voice, but I was slowly forgetting who it belonged to.

Looking up, my magic near full charge, I saw her.

Ozara…

I jumped away from her and screamed, "No!"

Finnegan still had partial control of my body, but I gained control of my magic and my mind. My hands took Ozara into them, not in a gentle way. Using strength that was not naturally mine, I threw Ozara against the far wall of rocks.

She fell to the ground and de-transformed, the magic flowing out from her fingers onto the ground.

She yelled and screamed in pain. The relic made her semi-immune to the pain, without its magic she felt everything she was experiencing.

You can fight it, Tristan! Her voice came over me.

"Ozara!" I grabbed at my head, a pounding filling it.

My father's mind was a part of my mine, and as I tried to use it to my advantage, a thought came to mind as the rocks fell from the ceiling. Gems also fell shattering to the ground, but one did not. It simply fell and bounced to the ground before me.

I reached my hand out to it, lighting it with my magic.

Emerson's relic...

Good and evil fought over my being, but both won. I landed onto the ground and met my father's eyes, something I had never done before.

"Don't make another move towards her."

~ ~ ~

Ozara's POV:

My whole body burned and ached. My skin was on fire, and I bit my cheek until I tasted blood.

Tristan had become a hybrid being with unimaginable power. I watched him as he floated in the air. One part of his body was lifted with a white wing and the other, a black one, flapping in sync with each other. A horn came from one side of his head, and his eyes glowed green with a trail of mist coming from them.

He was radiating magic energy, more magic energy than was safe for normal magic users.

He held his hand up, a sword being created from the air.

Finnegan rose from his pile of gems and went to Tristan, but Tristan blocked him with a shield of magic.

The collision was explosive, sending each of them into opposing walls.

Tristan's eyes met his father, and his father began to reach towards his head, fighting against an invisible force.

"Playing with other's thoughts doesn't seem fair, does it?" Tristan rose, dusting debris off him.

With super speed, his wings carried him from the ground and allowed him to push Finnegan to the ground and stab the sword through his exposed chest.

He rose, back up and fell to his knees.

"Tristan…" I slowly approached him, limping and wincing with each step.

He looked back at me, and my heart shattered.

The magic melted from him as he de-transformed. Tears were flooding from his eyes as he wept.

I limped to him and took him into my arms.

"Thank the heavens you are alright." I whispered, in disbelief of what had happened.

He clutched me tight, burying his head in my shoulder.

"Please… never let me become that monster again. Good and evil were fighting and… evil almost won. Please… promise me, Ozara that if I ever become that monster… I beg you to kill me."

"No." I shook my head, knowing he could feel it against his shoulder, "I could not kill you… You are the one person I can't lose."

We stood together, clinging to each other for what seemed like ages.

"How did you do it? You got him to fight himself one time… how?"

He sighed, leaning heavily against me, "I showed him the one thing he can't face… my mother. At least his last memory was of the woman he once loved."

After he had completely calmed down, he released me, coughing as the final effects of the fight subsided.

"Ozara… I think he always had a grip on my mind, because now that he doesn't… I don't think this is how I imagined freedom." He took an unsteady breath, "I've never felt so light, yet there is a heaviness in my chest… he was my father, my hero, before his beast took over his soul."

I wiped a single, final tear from slipping down his cheek.

"I hope I will never be weak enough to think my beast is the only way out."

I settled my hand on his cheek and met his eyes, noticing the magic swirling within them.

"One battle at a time, Tristan… one battle at a time."

~16~

THE SUN WAS just rising over the horizon, making the forest behind us a silhouette against it. On one side of me, deep blues and purples blended beautifully with the darkness of the night, sprinkled with a few stars. The other, faded between oranges and pinks, letting purple clouds dance around the sky.

"Wow…" My voice was only a breathless whisper.

Before I could really savor the moment, hoofbeats quickened behind us from the elven warriors. We were lucky to collect our belongings and escape the palace before the guard accepted the old man's rumor.

Nero's stride quickened as we plunged out of the forest. As Asmund steered the stallion through the tall grass of the valley, I tightened my grip around his waist.

"Hold on! I don't need you falling off." Asmund called over the wind rushing in my ears.

Rolling my eyes, even though he could not see me, I retaliated, "Yes, because that makes it so much easier." I enjoyed our moments of banter, though they were short lived.

The gallant steed easily carried us both through the open field, but it was clear to me he was not running at his full speed.

With two ears forward, Nero sped up, enjoying the open space.

A loud roar sounded through the clear air. Nero tossed his head and pulled on the reins.

The elven guards stopped at the edge of the forest, but I saw them turn back into the forest through stray pieces of hair that whipped in the wind.

"They are turning back."

We continued on through the tall grass as Asmund slowed Nero, allowing him to pace in circles as we watched the surroundings.

"Something isn't right…" He mumbled.

I felt the same thing he did but did not want to risk staying in the open. The air was too still for my liking, causing chills to encase my body and the hair on my neck to stand on edge.

I reached forward and took my sword from the scabbard attached to the saddle.

"We should leave." I placed my free hand on his shoulder.

Asmund nodded and urged Nero forward but the stallion refused to move.

"What is he doing?" I asked.

Asmund swore under his breath, "He did this when we first arrived. He won't move without being led."

I dismounted, tying up my dress for better range of motion before attaching my scabbard back to my hip.

Asmund took hold of Nero's reins and pulled him forward, resulting in head tossing from Nero.

The ground began to shake beneath us. Asmund offered an arm to steady me.

"We could make it on foot if we hurry." Keeping his back against mine, Asmund suggested and watched the space.

I shook my head, "We are already returning without a fallen comrade, I refuse to return without another."

I could hear the anger rising in his voice, "He is a horse!"

"Look him in the eyes, Asmund," I challenged, "He is intelligent and clearly has a personality. We are not leaving without Nero, unless you wish to explain to Milku how we left her prized steed in the grasp of the elven guards."

Amid our argument, the ground began to shake, causing me to lose my balance. Asmund quickly swooped in and caught me.

Dusting the dirt from my stolen dress, I glared up at him and pushed a piece of long hair from my face. By this point I was tired of the fancy clothes and longed for my chest piece to hide my insecurities.

A gust of wind blew through the valley, sending my hair swirling around my face.

A rustle in the bushes of the Sacred Forest, turned our attention back to it. The ground began to shake in closer intervals.

Patches of fur began to appear out of the trees as a giant creature emerged from them.

Not even being able to see the whole creature who stood nearly as tall as the pines it was emerging from, Nero ran off to the forest. And with him, he took our last option for escape.

The creature was tan in color with a dark stripe starting from his nose and trailing down to its nubbed tail. From the look of it, it seemed like a badger-like creature with a snout that was equally as long as his claws that were tiling up the dirt.

It lifted its head to the brightening sky, and let out a shrill scream, before making its way to us.

Each step made the ground shake more.

Asmund ran toward it, sword drawn, and I continued in his lead, abandoning my uncomfortable shoes in the tall grass.

Before Asmund could get an attack in, the creature lifted its large paw and hit him with the back of it. Filled with an amount of adrenaline I had never felt before, I changed my direction and ran to him.

I slid down next to him, "A-Asmund?" I cried.

He wiped his hand over his face, "I'm alright, just give me a minute." His eyes closed again, and he clutched his head.

Stop hiding your magic… A sing-song voice whispered in the wind which blew across my skin, encasing it in chills.

My eyes went wide as I glanced up at the large paw coming down on us. As an instinct, I threw my hands over my head, thankful my magic reacted as it did.

A dome of magic encased us, pushing the creature's paw away from us.

"Asmund! You have to get up!" I screamed, feeling my magic strain under the weight of the beast.

I heard him shift behind me, but I did not focus on it. My magic had given way, leaving us defenseless against the large paw.

As the paw was nearing us at a rapid pace, I felt a large shove to my back. I opened my eyes to the underbelly of the creature, feet away from where its paw would have crushed us.

My eyes went to Asmund who was standing over me. His eyes glowed with a still darkness, and the silver specks fading in and out behind it. His vest had been torn off, exposing a dirt stained, flowing shirt he wore beneath it. Blackness coated his hands and reached up his arms, a stain of magic pushing to be freed after lying dormant so long. Large wings full of black feathers ripped through the fabric on his back, and extended out completely.

The ground began to shake again as the creature moved from over us.

"Asmund!" I yelled over the noise of the beast.

As he turned to me, his eyes did not hold the same softness they once did. They were full of dark, beautiful magic that was slowly taking control of him.

Sunlight highlighted the dark undertones of his black hair as it peaked underneath the creature.

He has one thought in his mind... protecting you. It seems you are allowing history to repeat itself... The voice in my head warned.

Before I could say something to Asmund, his wings lifted him from the now open spot and he began to fight the creature.

As I watched him, a terrible sorrow gripped my chest. His magic was that of death, meaning in the end, this beautiful creature would die with no chance of moving on.

I ran to Asmund, knowing my prediction could not happen. Upon reaching him, I threw a blast of magic to push him back. He was not aware of what he was doing or how his magic would affect the ecosystem of this area. I threw another blast, knowing it did not hurt him with the strength of the relic protecting him.

After a few more blocks destroying his attacks, his attention would still not focus on me. He was determined to kill this creature.

Eventually, the creature was fed up with Asmund's magic and smacked him out of the sky.

Asmund somersaulted through the air, but still managed to land on his feet, creating deep ruts in the soft earth as he slid away.

The creature now stared at me, and I knew there was no escape. When I looked into its eyes I saw intelligence, similar to the look in Nero's. It saddened me to watch this creature be forced to become aggressive because of us. My magic begged to be freed, but I had used too much already.

The creature stepped up to me, making slow movements. Our eyes locked and something familiar lingered in its large doe eyes.

Then the voices came.

"FREE US!" They screamed.

Around me the people faded in and out as my magic fought against itself.

I removed my sword, preparing to fight them off this time. I stole my eyes from the beast.

The people crowded around me. Their gray bodies haunted me like a bad dream.

Journey! A familiar voice screamed among the crowd as I pushed a person off me.

I swung my sword, the blade coming close to the creature who watched me with horrid eyes.

Journey, no! The voice yelled again.

I heard the creature's paw leave the ground, and I spun to protect myself, holding my sword ready to attack.

No!

Piper appeared in front of me, her blonde hair hanging down to her waist, and her forest green eyes sparkling. She was how I remembered her so long ago. Visions burned my mind, while pain burned my skin as the creature's paw destroyed Piper's image and sliced its claws across my chest. In the darkness that came, visions filled my head of a life that was not mine to live.

"You must never harm the Guardian of the Forest. He protects us every day as we sleep." A woman looking strangely like Piper walked hand in hand with a young girl.

"He crosses from his forest to ours every dawn to watch over us. Then every dusk he returns to his den to rest."

The young girl smiled up at the woman, innocent joy shining in her forest eyes.

The Guardian walked up to them, the girl trembling in her steps. The woman began to hum a melody lost in the back of my mind, as the creature fell into her trance, and rested its snout against her hand.

"The Guardian will never harm you, Piper. He is our friend."

Tears burned in my eyes, hearing the last of my sword fall to the ground with a thud and whispered a silent apology.

I do not mean to hurt anyone… I am sorry, Piper.

~ ~ ~

Asmund's POV:

Seeing Journey fall from the claws of the beast, sent a wave of shock through me. I had lost who I was, making her feel the need to stop me.

Journey crumbled to the ground, three slash marks ingrained into her skin, blood seeping quickly down the fabric of her torn dress. She had not even screamed.

My wings lifted me from the ground and carried me to her with lightning speed.

As I landed beside her, I noticed the magic draining from her skin, the best indication of a magic user on the brink of death. She faded in and out of her Mystics form and as she did, I noticed the thousands of people flashing around us, their gray bodies lingering close.

"I'-m sorry…" Her voice dropped off.

Laying my ear to her chest, I froze from the silence.

I took her into my arms, "No…"

I caressed her cheek, feeling her body go limp in my arms, "Please, no!"

The wind blew over us, and I looked up to the large creature, reaching its paw up again.

I hung my head and held Journey close, not caring of the creature or its intent on hurting me.

My black hair began to stick to my face, which was coated in tears as my shoulders shook with silent sobs.

I had screamed, I yelled for her until I could not any longer, but still I whispered.

"No... please, no..."

The wind blew again humming a melody in its whispers. A calming song filled the air, making a small bit of peace wash over me.

The creature dropped its paw, causing the ground to shake beneath us. I watched it step towards us from through the feathers on my wing blocking us from one another.

Her snout reached to us, but as I watched, I realized its focus was not on us.

I folded my wing to my back, and froze, eyes wide.

The elf, I saw on her death bed, the elf I saw collapse in the ballroom stood before us, singing and holding her hand to the creature.

The wind blew over us, melting my magic from my body as it did with the spirits.

The elf and the large creature began to fade with the wind. They dissipated into nothing but stray magic in the air. This magic blew through Journey's hair, leaving gold dust tangled in her curls.

As the last of the creature disappeared in the wind, Journey took an uneasy breath.

Listen... The breeze blew cold against my skin.

An unsteady beating filled my ears. Quickly, I placed my ear back to her chest, and a heartbeat filled my ears. I clung to her, tears streaming down my face as I buried it in her tangled hair.

The last of my magic faded away as I realized, though the magic had given life to her, it was not enough to heal her wounds. My hands were coated in the red substance, which seeped faster through the fabric of her dress. Black feathers littered the ground stained with her blood.

I collected some of the feathers and used the shaft to pierce the fabric of my sleeve. After doing this a few times, I took the torn fabric and knotted them together before wrapping Journey's wound with it. It was not the best medicine and would not hold long.

The air went still again and I let out a shrill whistle.

"Nero!" I hollered, letting it echo across the valley.

Within an instant, the white horse peeked through the trees. Twigs were tangled in his mane and his white legs were stained with mud. He was only a bit spooked overall.

I whistled again, watching as he came trotting in response. When he arrived, he lowered his head and snorted at the ground.

"It's alright, big guy." I patted his sturdy neck.

I lifted Journey into my arms and laid her gently across his neck, making sure Nero would stand her weight while I mounted.

As usual, he stood still as a rock as I mounted. I positioned Journey so she was leaning on me, with my hand around her to hold her up, but also held pressure on her wound. After maneuvering us all to a semi-comfortable seat, I gathered some of Nero's mane and softened my reins ever so slightly.

"Alright, Nero. Now's your chance to run as fast as you can."

His ears flicked forward as I gave him a small nudge to the side. He shot forward with unnatural speed, still allowing me to remain in control.

He knew as well as I did, Journey's life had been spared from death, and we were not to be the ones to steal her second chance at life.

Her life was in our hands now.

~17~

THE TOWN HAS begun to crumble because of me. Althea refuses to admit it, but everything I touch breaks apart until it is nothing. This was not the magic I was intended to have.

And now in this place she has created for me, it is tainted with the darkness I have developed.

I didn't mean to hurt anyone... I didn't mean to cause the pain I have. If only I could have taken the pain and felt it for everyone, but I can't. I cannot be stopped, which is why I am here, looking into her beautiful green eyes as she hesitates to take my relic. Tears stream down her eyes, resulting in my own. How I wish I could take her into my arms, but I cannot risk the darkness infecting her.

We both had to do what was best for our people. What a cruel world. Sentencing two people who loved each other to be apart from one another. For one to be taken too soon and the other never being able to reach them. Our people came first, the price every hero must pay. But what she doesn't know is the prophecy that was given to me as my magic was manipulated. The words that repeated in my head all the days I was away from this world. And even now, I cannot bare to tell her. I shall take this secret to my grave.

As long as I live, people will continue to die.

~ ~ ~

Calvin's POV:

The air was too quiet, but I was lucky, enough that it filled my brother's unsteady breaths to keep him alive.

He began to shake, possibly from something the medics refer to as shock. I took my cloak from my shoulders and covered him with it. The seal of my kingdom being stained with blood.

"Seems like a fitting analogy…" I mumbled under my breath.

"When father died, it seemed the kingdom would be broken. You had run off, and I was forsaken by the people. Rumors began to cover the city with doubt of me. The people began to abandon me in pursuit of the crown. Just like him, they only wanted you. I was merely the outcast… the unwanted child."

I cleared my throat of the building tears, "I did everything right… I trained, I planned, but in the end, he still only wanted you. I was only heavy baggage on his shoulders. Yet still I was the only son at his funeral. The entire kingdom came to mourn, everyone he ever cared for…" I paused and looked over my younger brother, exhaling slowly.

"Except for you… you abandoned them, and he still chose you…"

~ ~ ~

Dear Journey,

Things have only gotten worse here. The Mystics' Tree has changed once again. Only this time, darkness has encased it.

The people have begun to riot and fight with the magic users, who become weaker by the day.

The guard has been sent to fight off the people, but the queen, being the coward, she is, refuses to do anything more.

August speaks of the horrors when he comes home each night. They have begun to point the blame to the old townspeople, and it has turned into a feud between the two sides of the kingdom.

The guards, who are witnessing this unfold, are thankful to come home to their families each night. I have hosted many over the past few days, as the guards are worried for their safety being alone. We live on the outskirts and miss much of the fighting that happens in the heart of the kingdom. Things are quickly getting out of hand.

I went searching through Piper's cottage for some ingredients I did not have and found the journal under the loose floorboard in your room. When I read it, I realized the true danger you were all in, but it is also acting strange. When the Tree changed its color, the journal began to glow, and more ink appeared on its pages. Do not worry, I have it in my possession and it is safe with me.

Considering what is happening here and the revelations in the journal, I truly believe it is in your best interest to not return to Secret Hollow.

~Celeste

~18~

I CLUTCHED THE bandage wrapped around my torso and arm as Celeste helped me pull my pink shirt over them without ruining the bandage or aggravating the wound.

"I am glad you are recovering." Celeste murmured to me as she removed the braids from my hair and wound it in a single braid.

"It has only been a few days; I have much more recovering to do."

Celeste placed her hand on my shoulder, "According to Asmund, you moved on from this world. Do not push yourself beyond your limitations."

"None of us fully understands what happened to me." I took a painful seat in a chair that was nearby, struggling to catch my breath.

Celeste let out a heavy sigh, "What did you see?"

"Do not sound so excited. I saw Piper's memories. How her mother became the Guardian of the Forest when the Elders sacrificed her to it. Asmund says the creature- I mean… Piper's mother gave her magic to heal me."

I took an unsteady breath, "No one but Asmund believes me, and I do not wish to explain why, but I saw her. Not through some light in my mind or as a moment of enjoyment when taking my last breath. I *saw* her."

Before Celeste could respond, a knock sounded on the front door of her home.

Celeste rose, peaked through the small window, and let Tristan, Ozara, and Asmund in.

Asmund hurried towards me and knelt before the chair, trying to meet my eyes.

"Thank the Heavens you are alright." He lifted my chin to meet his gaze.

I had been hesitant after seeing what happened on the outskirts of the Sacred Forest. I met his eyes, and smiled silently, enjoying the return of silver specks dancing in his eyes.

Asmund looked back to Celeste, "Is she well enough to return to Piper's cottage?"

"I honestly believe you could have taken her at any time, but I worry because of the townspeople. They want to kill her. They want to kill all of you."

"That is why we all came," Ozara spoke up, "To make sure that she had the protection and care she needed."

Ozara came often, and she spoke briefly of their time in Everwinter, without entering too much detail as the Leaders Alliance over Kocala and Resmen were not very happy with them.

"I still fear it will not be enough. Riots have been breaking out in the streets over all of you. Especially considering you all disappeared before it happened."

"We still must go." I spoke up, but still remained rather quiet.

The entire room went silent as they listened to me, "I know I have lied to all of you, and put you in this immense danger, but I believe it was meant to be us all along. We cannot hide ourselves from the world when it is the world that needs us."

"They *needed* us. They do not anymore." Tristan challenged.

"They are still our people," I paused, all of the built-up anger and hurt coming out at him, "You are the only one among us who chose their relic, you were not sentenced to this. Therefore, you should have considered the responsibilities that would be placed on your shoulders the same as the rest of us."

"I chose it to save our lives. I care not for these people, or what they do to destroy each other."

"Tristan!" Ozara spoke, "Stop your nonsense and put your beast to rest."

Tristan took a few deep breaths before speaking again, "I apologize, Journey. I didn't mean to come off as harsh, but you must realize sooner or later. These people do not want the Mystics anymore. We cannot convince them otherwise."

"Then I choose to learn it later."

Asmund stood and moved beside me, "We can worry about the people later. Right now, we need to get Journey somewhere she can rest without intruding on Celeste and Augustus. HE already does not appreciate us crowding in his home."

"Oh, please. It has been no issue. She is much more pleasant than the families of the guard we have been housing." She responded.

Ozara turned to Celeste, who was sitting at her small wooden table in the corner, "Guards' families never stay with one another unless they are in danger."

"As I said the people have begun to start riots and the guards worry about leaving their families alone."

I met Celeste's warm eyes, "You said things were getting worse, but are they really that bad?"

"Worse… and I understand why now." She paused, running her fingers through her orange curls, "I went searching in Piper's cottage for ingredients when I stumbled upon the Journal. I took it, thinking I could protect it… especially after what I read in it-"

"Has everyone read this journal but me?" Asmund cut her off.

"Perhaps you should tell them…" Celeste suggested.

I nodded and faced my new group, realizing we were brought together for a reason. We were all drawn to each other from the beginning.

"When Azguard was hit with that spell, the one that changed his magic, a prophecy was given to him, meant for Althea. As long as Azguard was alive, people would continue to die."

"Then why would the rest of the Mystics die after he did?" Tristan questioned.

"Because the relic was still activated. Only after it went dormant did everything stop." Asmund answered.

"I believe if the people were to realize this, they would try to kill all of you and destroy the relics. They do not want this to happen again. They want to make the Mystics extinct." Celeste explained.

"Then I will take the Journal and keep it hidden. Just like before." I offered.

Celeste hung her head, and in an apologetic tone, she admitted, "The journal has been stolen."

~ ~ ~

We left Celeste's home with our senses on high alert. I leaned heavily on Asmund, as my legs were still weak from the amount of blood I lost.

Tristan was behind us, and Ozara to my other side. Finding our way through the winding back streets posed an issue, but few people stopped to stare or cause commotion. As we continued down the street, I noticed many people whispering or closing the shutters to their houses. This was no longer the welcoming kingdom I once knew. I once loved.

Then the crowd began to draw. People kept their distances, yet still peeked around the buildings or through their windows.

Tristan was already tense from earlier, and I could feel his magic on edge.

The distinct sound of running footsteps came toward us, and we all looked to see a large, heterochromia, black wolf running our way.

Determination and fear filled Kova's eyes and his teeth were bared, allowing his panting breath to create white smoke in the air.

Within one quick move, Tristan covered us with one black and one white wing. I saw Kova lunge before Tristan blocked my view.

I heard a whimper followed by a large thud, and finally a gasp from the crowd.

As Tristan removed his trembling wings from around us, I lifted my hand to cover my gaping mouth.

Through tear blurred vision I saw Kova laying on the ground, with an arrow in his side. He was sitting in a pool of blood and coughing it onto the cobbled streets.

Basil shoved her way through the crowd and threw herself beside her brother.

Silent tears streamed down her dark face as her brother's blood stained her white hair. She did not say a word.

"Tristan, get Journey out of here, I'm going to get Celeste."

Tristan nodded to Asmund, and slung his arm around me, his wing blocking my view from the horrid scene.

I allowed him to lead me away, though my thoughts wandered back to the middle of the street, and what the people thought of the recent events.

My thoughts subsided and my heart broke when we reached the outskirts of the kingdom.

A lone howl filled the air.

~19~

HOW CAN ONE *find peace in a world where your mind has complete control? Voices that haunt you, and never leave. His voice is one of those voices.*

Kill them...

Kill them all and laugh at their suffering...

Even thinking of him fills my fading body with shivers.

I have been contemplating on Althea. After I leave, she will be the only one left. And as we have not taken any apprentices, I fear this generation of the Mystics will be the last. I have decided to give Althea more time.

Time... if only we could have had more time. But more time means pain.

Hopefully Althea will use this time to find heroes worthy of our magic. If she does not, I hope at least our story continues on in the hearts of those who loved us.

I can feel my magic slipping away from this world. How there were so many things I wish I could have made right. But how do you right the wrongdoing of taking lives… I do believe I could not.

Forgive me.

~ ~ ~

Calvin's POV:

Time had begun to drag on. Damon had been getting worse, his breathing labored, but he still was holding on more than most.

"This is what I wanted. Isn't it?" I asked aloud to myself.

"No… I only wanted to be a son worthy of his father's love… A king worthy of his kingdom… Someone worthy of happiness…" A tear finally slipped down my cheek as I watched my brother lying, slowly fading from this world.

My leg began to bounce up and down as sobs overtook me. I ran my fingers through my hair and screamed.

"Why?" I yelled, "Why… am I like this?"

"Why…"

I crossed to my brother and knelt before him, taking my sword from its scabbard, its tip still dripping with his blood. Using my magic to put an immense amount of force behind it, I struck it into the floor. Marble shattered around it, sending cracks across the entire room. I bowed my head, unable to let go of the sword's hilt.

"Could you ever forgive me… Brother…"

~20~

DARKNESS COVERED THE forest as the sun fell beneath the horizon. The lights strung in the trees were some help, but it seemed like no amount of light could lead me to the end of this long dirt road.

There was an ending. A quaint cottage with no inhabitant sat in the middle of a clearing in the small woods.

An off-white stucco made up the walls, supported with dark wood beams matching the tiling of the roof. A door was also made of the same wood, with a small glass window in the center. Vines and ivy grew up each wall and camouflaged it into the forest. The dirt path led right to the door and the grass surrounding it was coated with wildflowers as it was nearing spring in the region.

"Journey." Asmund's voice stole my attention, making me remember Tristan's silent reassurance left when he did.

"Sorry… I'm listening." I did not meet his eyes.

"It's… alright. Apparently one of the guards planned to assassinate you. He was tired of the fighting and thought killing you was the only way to end it. Kova knew of his plan… that's why he came to protect you."

"How many more will die because of me?" I was asking myself the question more than I was asking him.

He grabbed my uninjured hand and pulled me to a stop a few feet from the cottage.

"Why are you being so hard on yourself?" He turned me to look at him.

I refused to meet his gaze as I whispered, "Because I always have."

He placed his hand on my cheek and I leaned heavily into it, "You don't have to."

I offered a smile, "I just wish we could go back to the night when we first met. Everything was much simpler."

"I did not know starting a war was simple." He chuckled.

Fond of those memories, I smiled. Trying to read deep into them, I finally met his eyes.

"What do you remember of that time?"

He smiled, "I remember when we first met… my hands were shaking and I knew even then, though I didn't want to admit it to myself, you were going to change my life. What I didn't know was that you had already changed my life. You changed my life when I first found out you were alive. Because for the first time in my life, I wasn't alone."

With tears threatening to spill from my eyes, I wrapped my arms around his neck, thankful when he carefully wrapped his arms around my waist being considerate of my wounds.

"Please… if you cannot promise me anything else… will you promise me no matter what happens, you will always remember me." He whispered; his breath warm against my skin.

Quickly I pulled away, wincing as I did, "No… I've lost too many people to think of losing you." I paused, "Can't we just run away? Get away from this place for one night…"

"I thought you did not want to leave here."

I hung my head, "What if I do… this place… it just isn't home anymore."

"Because, the people keep hold on your heart." He smirked, pushing a curl of hair behind my ear, "I have to keep watch, I could not bear it if someone were to come for you, and me not be here to protect you."

He hugged me quickly, and I savored it, knowing at this point any moment could be our last.

As he held me in the protection of his strong arms, I did not think of Damon or Piper. And I finally realized why it felt right when I was in his arms.

Since the beginning, Damon had felt familiar to me. But each time Asmund's skin grazed mine or I lost my thoughts in the depths of his eyes, it felt as though two souls separated for eternity had been reunited.

They came together from all over the cosmos and finally found each other in us.

~ ~ ~

I closed the door to Piper's cottage, ignoring its creaking.

The entry covered with vines and overgrown plants was dark. I hung my cloak on the small pegs attached to the wall. Feeling for the small table by the door, I retrieved the candle and lit it, providing light for me to see the empty cottage.

Passing the stairs, I ran my hand along the banister, dust gathering on my fingertips. The bookshelf at the end of the hall was sagging in the middle of each shelf with books and scrolls. Piper enjoyed her days when she could take a moment to read. Those were her favorite days.

The entry opened into the living room. The same stucco on the outside made up the walls and fireplace on the far wall. Plants cluttered the mantle and their overgrown stems hung down the front. There was no fire lit… no warmth in the air. The coffee table was cluttered and unusable as usual, but

I slowly began to realize. While I saw it all as clutter, Piper knew where everything was.

The worn seating was covered with blankets sprawled about for winter, but never put away in the spring. Instead of paintings, bookcases full of plant clippings and journals sat against the wall. A desk stood quietly under the window on the back wall, which like everything was covered in various tools and plants.

I spun around and looked up to the landing of the stairs. In between the balusters sat small, individual plants that had grown to hang down the entrance of the living area.

My eyes wandered to the arch leading to the kitchen. It was pitch black besides the moonlight coming from the window. It was cold… lonely. There would be no more late-night talks to take place within those walls. The kind you can only have in the cover of darkness at night when everything became deeper.

I tore my eyes from the sight and around the furniture, taking a seat on the sofa.

I watched the candle dim and stared into the darkness with only the tiniest bit of candlelight to reveal what I once gazed naively over.

Sighing, the darkness slowly creeping in on me, I began to weep, revealing my true fear.

I was not afraid of being alone.

I was afraid of my thoughts being my only company.

~21~

Asmund's POV:

MY HEAD RESTED on the wall of Piper's cottage. My thoughts were racing, keeping me dazed from the noises of the night.

I cannot protect her… she will be in danger as long as the relic is active… they all will be.

I knew for some time, as my thoughts drifted to the scenario often, that I could never bear to lose her. And if I never wanted to, then I had one thing I must do.

I sighed and removed the gem from my pocket. The moment was still fresh in my head.

Journey dried her tears quickly and peered out of the room for our exit. As her back was turned, I looked down at the lost elf. A bright green stone sat on her still chest.

"I apologize, Your Majesty, but when you know what I will use it for, I feel you will forgive me." I whispered and slipped the gem from her neck.

We fled the castle with no trace of the missing gem.

The Sacred Gem was the wielder of the magic I had been looking for. With it and the magic from my relic, my plan should work perfectly.

Asmund... It called to me, beckoning to use its power for a selfish task.

I shoved it back in my pocket, *it's what I must do.*

The magic contained in the gem was enough to open the portal, and mine was enough to sentence Calvin and me to a place there was no moving on from. That place would offer no escape and no ability for my relic to surface again.

Still there was one thing I had to do before I left. My eyes fell to the paper in my lap. I pushed it against my knee and signed my name in the shaky font that was barely legible.

Rising from my seat on the ground, I checked to see if the candlelight had gone out, and to my luck… it had.

I slid the papers under the door and whispered a spell of protection over the cottage, keeping Journey from stopping me.

Finally, I plucked a feather from my pocket and slid it under with the letter.

I whispered to myself, "Goodbye, Journey."

~ ~ ~

Asmund's POV:

The town was deserted at this time of the night. The only people around were the guards on patrol.

I kept my head down, to not meet their gaze. My thoughts ran wild in my head.

Hopefully she will learn to be happy without me... with him, I am sure she will be fine.

I sighed, watching my breath swirl in the night air.

The moon seemed to guide me along the twisting streets that were hidden between rows of towering buildings. Laundry hung from lines over my head, not being affected by the little wind of the night.

If my memory served me correctly, the place to open the portal was near the center of New Hollow.

It was a beautiful place.

A fountain was placed in the center of the courtyard, cleaned of vines and debris. Strands of flowers came from each building and met at the top point of the fountain.

The townspeople spoke often of the events and dances held here.

With the streetlights reflecting on the clear water, I wished I had more time to experience this adventure with her.

But my mind was clear. If I was to stay around, there was the possibility she would die. And I could not allow that.

I lifted my hand to the night sky and whispered a single wish to the stars.

"Let her be happy without me."

My magic activated the gem and a bright light appeared in the center of the fountain, cracking the sides and spilling water over the cobbled streets.

The beautiful courtyard was destroyed as it expanded the full width of the portal.

All beautiful things must come to an end.

~ ~ ~

Damon's POV:

A wave of magic energy refilled the air, healing me of some pain from my wounds.

I had been fading in and out as Calvin was speaking. He seemed sincere in his storytelling as I had never imagined those events from his twisted point of view.

As I slowly opened my eyes, a brilliant light filled them, slowly eating away at the realm.

She has found us…

~22~

Asmund's POV:

PIECES OF MARBLE began to fall to the ground, exploding on impact. But I only had to wait. Eventually the magic of reversing the portal would destroy that realm and bring everything here.

Over the course of the next few minutes, the portal began to get smaller, leaving only remnants of the beautiful realm.

I knelt down for a moment and paid my respects for the souls of Azguard and Althea being freed from the confines of the realm.

As my eyes lifted, I spotted a figure standing and staring at himself, seeming grateful to be alive.

Anger began to coarse through my veins, and his ice blue eyes met mine.

"You?" Calvin yelled across the opening, removing a blood-stained sword from the rubble.

"I almost forgot about you…" He let out a premature laugh, "Not that you were much to remember."

I said nothing, but let the magic overtake me, pushing me past my limit.

The weight formed on my back and the gem in my hand turned black as my magic creeped up my skin.

With the gems leftover power, I created a small barrier around us, partly aware of what I was doing. Calvin began to back up, fear finally filling his eyes.

"You will never hurt anyone again." With unnatural speed, my wings lifted me from the ground and carried me to him.

I grabbed him by the collar of his shirt and lifted him into the air with me.

Without thinking the gem dropped to the ground, exploding as it struck the debris.

"It seems you have become just as evil as me." Calvin spit.

"No… love is not based on evil."

I knew he could feel my magic coming off in waves.

"The stone of death…" His eyes went wide, "Wait, please stop. You will sentence us beyond death with that magic."

"Maybe that was my plan all along." I said and released the magic within me."

~ ~ ~

Damon's POV:

I was pushed away by the magic of the barrier. I could only see the light of the magic being used.

Just when I thought I couldn't handle the power of magic, it disappeared. Followed by a loud explosion.

My eyes were coated with dust, but as I pried them open, I gasped at the crater trying to suck me into its depths.

At some point, as time was slipping away from me, people began to gather around the crater. Some were screaming or simply whispering about what could have happened.

"Damon!" A voice, I thought I would only hear in my dreams, carried through the crowd.

"Tristan, help me get him out!" I could have sworn she was an angel, coming to take me away from this horrid place, but she was real.

"Damon!" Her face appeared before me.

As her skin touched mine, the pain became lessened. After a few coughs I was able to speak.

"I-I'm alright… just please, help me sit up."

Quickly, Tristan and another woman from the crowd, leaned me against the wall of a building. The woman handed me a cloth for my wound and said the medic was on her way.

I nodded my thanks to her and looked to the destruction before me.

"Damon, w-where is Asmund…" Journey's pleading green eyes met mine.

I felt as though my throat was coated with dust, for it was too dry for me to speak.

Her voice turned urgent, "Please, Damon… where is he?"

Tears began to slip down my cheeks, "I'm sorry, Journey... so sorry..." I leaned my head against the wall and covered my face with my blood-stained hand, a sinking feeling filling my chest, "Asmund and Calvin... they're gone... they're both gone."

Journey stood up from beside me and cautiously climbed to the edge of the crater.

"No!" She screamed, "Please... no... not you too." She fell to her knees and wept, something I had a feeling she had been doing too often.

No, Calvin... I could never forgive you for the sins you have committed or the pain you have caused. You are not my brother, not the one I remember.

I watched Journey stand with a sword in her hand. As she stood, she became three people that struck the sword into the ground, the last memorial of a fallen warrior. She began to split apart and fade away. A faint blue light illuminated her silhouette.

It called to me.

Damon...

Then everything went dark again.

~23~

I SLID DOWN the door to Piper's cottage. Tears streamed down my face as I hugged his forgotten cloak to my chest.

This can't be real… please don't let it be real…

"Not you too…" My thoughts started to become reality.

I put my hands to my side, something crumbling underneath them.

My eyes wandered to the dark floor beside me. I lifted my hand to reveal wrinkled pieces of paper.

I allowed my magic to glow in my hand, illuminating the letter. The light cast a shadow of me, but it did not stop me from reading through tear-stained vision.

Journey,

I must apologize… because the things I say in this letter, you deserved to hear face to face, but time is not on our side.

I have already thought of what I am to do, as I have thought of it for some time now, but due to the recent news of the Journal, this is what I must *do. Yet, I still find myself thinking, "I will be away from you forever… how long will forever be?"*

I want to say so many things, but I am no good at writing… However, I must say, when you came across the room to me in the Sacred Forest, with that beautiful smile I missed so much, I honestly believe I fell in love with you.

And I recently have learned, it would be impossible to live without you. You have been a sense of peace, of home, through the chaos of my life, because I think I knew all along you were going to change my life.

I never told you, but when we first met, my hands were shaking, and I was terrified. Not only terrified of getting close to you, but terrified because I already knew I was going to.

I can control my choices… but I could not control falling for you. And it is hard to know you will read this when I am gone. Even mentioning the words makes me miss you. I already know as I am walking to where the portal will lay, my wish will be to turn around and come home to you, but I know I must not. I know as long as I am alive, you are in danger. Which is why I have made this decision. Where I am going, no one can find and activate the relic. You will be safe.

It is hard to move on with my story, knowing you will not be in it, but you were always stronger than me. You always tried to figure out everything before you went on, but I ask this one time that you move forward without having it figured out. There is no sane reason, none but the one in my head, for what I am about to do. I am scared... but love has made this a beautiful kind of fear.

For all this time, you were my light... I ask you to keep being the light for someone else. And should there be a day when you find yourself missing me, just take a breath, and smile. Then I at least know you smile when you think of me.

I know not who holds your heart, but my wish is they accept you. When you spoke of Damon in the Sacred Forest, I think you were trying to admit to yourself that he did not accept you. Given the second chance he has, I hope he learns to hold your heart as I can only wish I once did.

Do not cry for me, for you only deserve a life of happiness and peace. I want you to find that without me. Darling, you will become someone's best thing, as you are mine. Keep your head up, lest your crown should fall.

I promised to never leave you alone, and I have not. Legend says a black feather is a symbol that you are never alone, let it be your reminder of me…

With Love, Always,

Asmund.

Tears were streaming down my face, dripping onto the paper.

My magic began to rise in the pit of my stomach and burn on my hands.

I rose, letting the papers fall to the floor.

"Free us!" The voices began again.

I turned the corner to the kitchen and burst through the back door.

"FREE US!" They kept screaming.

I dunked my hands into the water basin outside of the door.

But they kept yelling, "Free us!"

You are hurt, Journey... the woman's voice appeared, *do not let the voices use you.*

"Free us... Free us." They chanted.

Finally, I yelled back, "Stop!"

I stood with tears dripping into the water basin, and whispered, "Just... stop."

And for the first time in months, everything went silent.

It was finally silent.

~24~

IT HAD BEEN three weeks since Asmund left me.

It had been three weeks since Damon almost lost his life but was saved thanks to the uncovering of Fredrick's relic which was hidden by the spell of the elves.

It had been three weeks since I had spoken to him, because I could not bring myself to do so.

"Perhaps you would like to venture outside today?" Celeste asked as she removed the last of the bandages.

I glanced at myself, in the mirror-like object in Piper's room.

I had grown pale from lack of sun and lost an immense amount of weight from refusing sleep and food. My hair was a tangled mess that could not hide the bags under my eyes. And my eyes… they were murky green and fogged over. It felt like I had taken a step back in time.

I noticed the large scars peeking from beneath my sleeve. They covered my arm and torso. I was…

"Journey? Celeste?" Are you two here?" A voice sounded from downstairs.

"We are upstairs, Ozara." Celeste called back.

The stairs creaked as Ozara climbed them and entered the room, still covered in her long cloak.

"Good afternoon, Ladies." Ozara looked at me, but I did not respond.

"I'll leave you two alone. Journey remember to wrap your wounds before you go to bed tonight."

I hung my head, "I do not sleep…"

"Do it anyway." She commanded with a serious look.

After Celeste disappeared around the corner, Ozara began to speak, "You know, Damon has been having a hard time adjusting." She took a seat on the trunk at the foot of Piper's bed.

"Is that so?" I asked, pulling my hair over my shoulder to braid it.

"Well the town has changed, he has lost his brother, became a relic user… oh, and the woman he loves refuses to speak to him. So, yes, I would say he has a good reason for not adjusting well."

"I am not refusing to speak to him, I just don't wish for him to see me like this." I sat in the chair across from her.

She tilted her head, her vibrant blue eyes studying me, "Why is that? What is wrong?" Her question was not a very smart one.

"I'm just having a bad day."

"Good try, but you have a lot of those. Try again."

Anger began to boil in my veins, "Do I need an excuse as to why I do not wish to see someone?"

A smile covered her face as she pushed her ash blonde hair into a ponytail, "There's the spirit you've been missing."

I took the black feather from the desk and spun it between my fingers.

"Look, Journey… I didn't come here to upset you, but it's been weeks and I really think you just need to talk about it."

"I-I don't even know what to say, mostly because I don't know how to feel about it. I can't decide whether I am mad at him for what her did, or thankful for the hope he gave me after Damon left…"

"I told him… I told him to take me back to the night we first met. How I wish I could go back to when everything was simple. When the stars shone above our heads the same as they shone in his dark eyes. And I want nothing more than to be able to look into his eyes again. H-How do you let go of someone like that? How do you let go of someone who made everything feel like an adventure, but made you feel at home at the same time?"

She chuckled, "What can I say? Your heart longs for adventure, but you love the feeling of home. I guess, to you, Asmund was the feeling of home that followed you on every adventure."

"I have learned, Journey, that grief is only love. Love that was never shown, never given a chance to become stronger. When the person you love is gone… you start to think of all the things you never said or did. You realize what you lost and how important they were to you. And grief is the only way to let go of that regret… that constant cry for him." She paused, leaning her elbows onto her knees.

"The older we get, the harder life becomes, because we lose more people. The more people we lose, the greater the pain becomes."

I stayed silent and let her continue.

"You are thinking of why you loved him, and the only answer you are finding is that you just loved him. Because every feeling you were too afraid to show, is coming out. You refuse to grieve; you are trapping that feeling in your heart when it needs to be released."

"I-I'm not ready to let him go."

"Then don't. Don't let him go… don't forget him. Make him a memory. One you will always keep with you. One you will think back on in hard times and smile at."

"There is no one who can heal your heart, Journey. Asmund's love for you was a special one.

He didn't give his life for you; he gave it for someone you care about. That takes immense strength."

I exhaled slowly, "I just wish I could tell him… say all of the things I never did. I mean, what if I never love again after him. I took the biggest risk of my life getting close to him, I don't think I could do that to myself again."

"You won't love anyone the same way you loved him, but that does not mean you will never love again. You will realize there is nothing to do but move on. Because one day, with or without him, everything will be okay. Pain… like the people who cause it, leaves."

I let my eyes wander down to my hands, "But what if this time… the pain doesn't go away."

"Eventually, you will allow yourself to grieve and the pain will go away."

I met her intense eyes, "How do you know of this?"

A small smile came onto her face, as if she was remembering something from a different time, "We all have someone we never speak of. And we will love them no matter what, but… sometimes we are given a second chance. It is our job to act on that chance."

"S-So, how exactly is Damon doing?" I finally asked.

She rose, placed her hand on my shoulder and smiled, "Why don't you go ask him yourself?"

~25~

SHIPS SWAYED AGAINST the sunset, leaving shadows on the once clear water of the docks.

It was nearly dark, and this was the one place of New Hollow that was not lit at night. It expanded the length of the old, white sand beach and held six ports which were taken up on this chilly night.

As I passed multiple sailors heading for town, I searched for the one man in particular.

I spotted him at the far end of the dock.

He was dressed in civilian clothing. A loose-fitting white shirt was unlaced at the top, revealing his bandage. A pair of beige pants held the shirt in place and were tucked into a pair of tall boots. His blond hair was messy and overdue for a trim, as well as the stubble that had appeared on his jaw. He clung to a walking stick to help the damage done to his leg and side muscles from his wounds.

"Damon!" I called to him, stealing his attention from the sunset.

His lapis eyes met mine, sparkling as they landed on me.

"Lady Journey... I-I apologize, it has been so long." He stated as I approached him.

I looked down at my feet, "I wish you would have been the one to cut that time short. I feel like it would have taken much less time to speak to you again."

"I wanted to give you the space you needed."

I glanced out over the water, "I am sorry we have not spoken."

He lifted my chin to see my face, "Just because I have not spoken to you, does not mean you have not been on my mind-" He paused and removed his hand from my face, "My apologizes... I know he holds your heart. And I know because of me, he is gone."

"It was not your doing... The world seems to reward me even when I do not deserve it... though I will not say his sacrifice was a reward."

He paused, "Whatever you think of what happened in Althea's Realm... whatever you think of me pushing you through the portal, I want you to know you were worth the sacrifice."

I remained quiet.

"Journey… I know you do not love me, at least not the way I love you. And I understand… you don't have to."

"But… I want you to know that I am yours. That's it, no expectations. This is not an over the top declaration of my love or my attempt to work myself into your heart. If all we are, if all we will ever be is friends, by heavens, even just a guard and townsperson, then I will be grateful for that. I just wanted to let you know if you need me, I'll be there."

His voice grew quiet, "It terrifies me to know I can look at you and know I would do anything for you, but I am willing to face that fear. If you knew the way I fell for you, you would understand how I could never fall for someone the same way. Honestly, a part of me will always be waiting for you."

I cleared my throat, "You once told me I was special… do you still believe it? B-Because I have ruined everything and in return, I have lost everything."

He placed his hands on my shoulders, "That is not true… you have not lost me," he paused, looking over my tear-stained face, "I'm here. Whether you wish to talk about what happened or not, I am here." He released me and began to limp away.

"Damon…" I turned after him, "I'm not ready to talk… but will you please stay?"

A smile came over his face, his lapis eyes sparkling, "Always, M'lady."

This time, hearing that word, I smiled, letting them be my happy memory. I walked up to Damon and linked my arm in his. He smiled down at me.

As we neared the edge of the marketplace at the front of the dock, I spotted August and Celeste coming toward us.

"Damon?" August took his arm from Celeste's and marched over to us.

"After everything," He began, "You still go back to her. How incompetent are you?"

"August!" Celeste gasped.

The red ring in his eyes began to expand, "You could die tomorrow by her hand and still defend her name."

Damon stood still, holding his pride in his stance, "And that would be my choice to make, would it not?"

"Can't you see that she is playing you? She probably isn't even upset about that man dying! She doesn't even care that he is dead because of her."

I began to tremble at his words, forgetting how to respond to August's anger.

"You need to leave August."

His anger flared, "Why? So, you can convince more people to fall into her web of lies! So, she can kill more people?"

Celeste went to take his hand, but it was too late, the red had already spread to the edge of his eyes, glowing with his dark magic. He threw her hand away.

"Ever since day one, she has been manipulating people. How many more people have to die, huh?"

He got much closer to us, and Damon moved to be between us.

By this time, the townspeople in the market gathered around and the guard had been alerted.

"When will you learn how much of a danger she is to all of us!" He was inches from Damon.

"Augustus!" A shrill voice pierced the night air.

August came to his senses, his eyes still red, and bowed to the queen.

"Oh, stop that and meet my eyes!" She commanded impatiently.

He met her mint eyes.

"Just what I thought. I heard the whole thing Augustus, and I have to say, I am very disappointed. The Captain of the Guard should not show the behavior you have tonight."

"I apologize, my Queen. It will not happen again."

"No, it won't because you are hereby relieved from your position of Captain. And for the safety of New Hollow and Secret Hollow alike, I also banish you from this land."

"But your Majesty!" He argued.

"Your behavior to the Prince of Evnock and our Guardian, Althea is inexcusable. We are to stand beside each other in our greatest time of sorrow." She met my eyes and we shared a silent moment between us.

She was beginning to learn the true meaning of being the Queen of Secret Hollow.

"Fine. Let's go, Celeste." He began to stomp away, but Celeste did not follow.

He turned back to her, "Come on, Celeste."

She hugged herself and played with the sleeve of her dress, "I will not be leaving with you, Augustus."

"What! You are my wife, you need me!" He yelled.

She met his eyes, "You are not the man I married! I am done apologizing for you August… I am tired of your manipulation. You are a grown man, and I expect you to act like one. I will not be leaving with you."

He scowled and spit at her feet, causing a gasp to come from the crowd. His soul was consumed with anger.

He shoved through the crowd into the depths of darkness.

Alone.

~26~

Ozara's POV:

I ANSWERED THE door and invited Damon into Milku's house.

"You summoned me." He smiled, nodding a thanks as he entered.

"Yes, I-I got a letter from Evnock."

He took a seat, "Evnock?"

I nodded, "From your mother… she wants me to return and become her commander again."

Damon jumped to his feet and patted my shoulder, "That is wonderful news, Ozara."

"Is it?" I met his eyes.

"You do not wish to return?"

I shook my head, "No, that's not it. I would love to return. Serving under Lady Ashton was my best moments of service. But… I don't know if I am ready to move on from this part of my life."

"What is keeping you here?" He questioned.

"Tristan."

He let out a small laugh, "Ozara, you are meant to wear a uniform. You are a wonderful commander and you love doing it. If Tristan really cares for you, then he will understand and support you in your decision."

I nodded, "There is another thing."

"Yes?"

"Lady Ashton is requesting your presence in Evnock. She wants you to come home."

~ ~ ~

Ozara's POV:

Tristan helped me take my last bag out of Milku's home. We said a quick goodbye to Milku and carried on our way through the streets of New Hollow.

"I still cannot believe you did not tell me Lady Ashton had asked you to return to Evnock." He stated as we took a corner, approaching the docks.

"I did not want to upset you. I love being here with you, but I left a part of myself in Evnock, a part that I also love."

And loving you is dangerous… I wanted to say, *I have more enemies than anyone should have. And because of that, it is not wise to have someone I care about.*

He looked away from me, "It was still your decision whether or not to accept the position."

But it was not my decision to fall for you.

I glanced at him, smirking at the pout on his face, knowing somewhere deep inside he was hurt, but he was not good at showing it, "Would you have stayed in Evnock with me, had I asked?"

I expected him to become flustered, but instead he grew serious, "No… I feel as though I am more needed here."

We were both silent as we shoved through the bustling crowd.

Eventually, I had to speak, "Will you come to visit?"

Entering under the gateway to the docks, he smiled at me, "Every chance I get."

Damon and Journey were waiting for us by the boat, smiles covering their faces.

"Are we ready?"

Journey nodded, looking much better than she did a week ago.

"Are you ready to go home?" I asked Damon.

He chuckled and looked to his feet before meeting my eyes, "I am already home. I am merely fixing a mistake I made many years ago."

They started up to the ship, but I stole one last glance at Secret Hollow, my home away from home.

~27~

EVNOCK'S DOCK WAS lined with boats as usual, but under the surface, the kingdom was still in high repair. Lady Ashton had been re-crowned as Queen and things seemed to be falling back into place.

As Damon and Tristan tethered the boat, I helped Ozara with her bags.

I recognized an older woman standing towards the back of the docks, peering over the heads of the many people. She had changed considerably, but she could not be mistaken.

Her black hair was cut short, and her lapis eyes sparkled bright. She gained a good amount of weight and looked healthy in her simple clothing.

Damon lifted his head and spotted her, "…Mother?"

She spotted him at nearly the same time, and took off for him, leaving her guards in shock.

He took her into his arms and hugged her tightly, clinging to her as if he never had.

Lady Ashton shook with sobs and clung to her son, afraid to let him go again.

We stood by watching them hold each other, all of us too mesmerized to break them apart.

I wiped a tear from slipping down my cheek and smiled.

"It seems like things are finally being made right." Ozara placed her hand on my shoulder.

I met her eyes, "I think to Lady Ashton, it was never wrong. She loves her son, that will never change."

~ ~ ~

We were whisked away to the castle, which was still under repair from the war. It took Evnock much longer to recover, because they were buckling under Calvin's weight for much longer. The people needed to heal just as much as the kingdom.

"I am so excited you have returned to us, Ozara. Evnock has not felt the same without you." Lady Ashton, whose arm was linked in Damon's, spoke.

Ozara nodded, "Yes, I am happy to be back. I certainly missed serving under you."

We walked by a damaged area of the kingdom that had not been demolished and rebuilt yet. A whipping post sat silent, no life around it. But I saw them, the lonely people gathering around, waiting for their second chance.

I made the images leave my mind, "I am sorry about Calvin, Lady Ashton." I felt like I had to be the one to say it.

She sighed, "He was my son, yes, but I lost him long ago. I hope wherever he is, that he is learning from his mistakes."

"He really did love this kingdom, Mother. To him, it was the only thing he had left."

She nodded, changing from the subject of her fallen son, "And you, Journey… I heard you also lost someone close in the defeating of my son."

"Yes, I may not feel him with the magic I possess, but in my heart, he will never be gone."

"And you are doing well?"

I offered a smile, "Better than I was."

"And what about you, Mother? Have you been doing well?" Damon asked, speaking mostly of her recovery.

She hesitantly nodded, "Yes... it has been a struggle, but I am slowly rebuilding myself with the rebuilding of this kingdom. As you can tell, I am beginning from the ground up, just as your Father did."

"You will not be doing it alone. Secret Hollow is willing to form an alliance that we believe was broken long ago, and you will always find an ally with the Mystics." I spoke around Damon.

She nodded, "I have heard the people of Secret Hollow do not take kindly to you." She stated bluntly.

My eyes wandered to the ground before I met her eyes, "Times have changed since Althea was here."

Nodding her agreement, she whispered, "That they have."

~28~

OZARA HELD ONTO Tristan longer than usual, lingering for a moment.

"Your mind is made up that you will return to Secret Hollow?" Lady Ashton asked Damon.

He nodded, "Yes, Mother. My calling is to protect, and at this moment in my life, my loyalty lies with Journey. It is my job to protect her."

Lady Ashton's eyes sparkled, "I have a feeling that role will be switched in due time."

I glanced over to Ozara and Tristan, as Ozara spoke, "Promise you will write to me every so often?" She asked as she finally pulled away from his embrace.

Tristan laughed, "Of course, Ozara."

She lifted her hand to his cheek, smiling when he placed his over hers, "Take care of yourself… and keep that beast of yours under control."

A somber look came over Tristan's face, "I will try my hardest."

"That is all I ask." She gave him a quick peck on the cheek before turning to stand with Lady Ashton, a smirk covering her face.

Tristan's face turned red as he looked out to the sea.

"You will come to visit, won't you?" Lady Ashton questioned Damon who was standing beside me.

"Of course, Mother. I have a feeling we will all be returning very soon."

I was the last to load onto the ship, taking one look back at Lady Ashton and Ozara.

We stood together and waved to those on the dock, until they became only dots in the distance. I crossed the swaying ship to the front and leaned heavily on the front mast.

We were heading back to Secret Hollow, back to an unknown future.

Tristan had been right many weeks ago.

The Mystics were complete, but our generation was unwanted. So, we did what any people would… one by one, we continued on with our lives. Not as the Mystics. But as Ozara the Commander, Tristan the Beast Slayer, Damon the Guard, Asmund the Sacrificed, and me… Journey, the Broken Angel.

~Acknowledgements~

Thank you to everyone who made this book possible. That includes you, the reader. Whether you have read my other books or not, I hope this book has taken you on an adventure and shown you that even broken angels can fly. And that anyone can be a light to another. Be the light you want to see in this world.

To my parents, once again you have supported me through another crazy project of mine. We are learning together and without your love and support, I would never be where I am today. I hope I have made you proud.

To my friends, you know who you are, and you know that I would not be the same person I am today without you. I've known some of you for what seems like forever, and others, only a short time, but you have all made an impact on my life.

To my bullies, my first book was my reassurance of my strength, but this one is fulfilling my dreams. You all still haunt me like the people in this story, but the people around me, my closest friends and family are showing me how to combat it. I am moving on, but I would have never started writing without you, so, thank you.

To Mrs. V.H., you have stuck through it all and pushed me to be open with my writing. I hope you are proud to see, slowly I am making that wish a reality. You have made me not only a better writer but a better person in both character and faith.

And to God, My Heavenly Father, You have placed me on this earth for a reason, for a purpose. You have a plan that is beyond my understanding, and I am enjoying watching it unfold. Every time I doubt, you show me why I should trust You. I have had my ups and downs, but You have been there the whole time. I pray this novel reaches the people You need it to reach, and with Your grace that I change the world. Even if it is only one person's world. And even if that person is me.

~About The Author~

Tacori Bean lives with her parents, horse, and three dogs in the suburbs of North Alabama. She found her love for writing as a light at the end of a dark tunnel and felt that God called her to help others through her stories. When she isn't in school or writing, she spends time reading, horseback riding, playing with her three pups, or finding new ways to express her creativity. She published her first book at 15 because she believes anyone who wants to write, can write.

Find out more about the life of a teenage author at Tacori Bean, Author on Amazon, YouTube, Facebook, and Instagram.

Made in the USA
Columbia, SC
07 August 2020